A. E. Hotchner

The Amazing Adventures of Aaron Broom

A. E. Hotchner is the author of the interna-
tional bestsellers *Papa Hemingway*, *Doris Day:
Her Own Story*, *Sophia*, and his memoir, *King of
the Hill*. He has adapted many of Hemingway's
works for the screen, and he is the founder, with
Paul Newman, of Newman's Own.

The Amazing Adventures of Aaron Broom

The Amazing Adventures of
Aaron Broom

A Novel

A. E. Hotchner

ANCHOR BOOKS
A Division of Penguin Random House LLC
New York

FIRST ANCHOR BOOKS EDITION, JUNE 2019

Copyright © 2018 by A. E. Hotchner

All rights reserved. Published in the United States
by Anchor Books, a division of Penguin Random House LLC,
New York, and distributed in Canada by Random House
of Canada, a division of Penguin Random House Canada
Limited, Toronto. Originally published in hardcover
in the United States by Nan A. Talese/Doubleday,
a division of Penguin Random House LLC,
New York, in 2018.

Anchor Books and colophon are registered
trademarks of Penguin Random House LLC.

The Library of Congress has cataloged
the Nan A. Talese/Doubleday edition as follows:
Names: Hotchner, A. E., author.
Title: The amazing adventures of Aaron Broom : a novel /
A. E. Hotchner.
Description: First edition. | New York : Nan A. Talese, 2018.
Identifiers: LCCN 2017025535
Classification: LCC PS3558.O8 A68 2018 |
DDC 813/.54—dc23
LC record available at https://lccn.loc.gov/2017025535

Anchor Books Trade Paperback ISBN: 978-0-525-43653-9
eBook ISBN: 978-0-385-54359-0

Book design by Maria Carella

www.anchorbooks.com

Printed in the United States of America
10   9   8   7   6   5   4   3   2   1

I dedicate this book
and the indomitable spirit of Aaron Broom
to the brave children
of the Hole in the Wall Gang Camp.

The Amazing Adventures
of Aaron Broom

Olive where it comes into Tenth is very busy, what with the streetcars crisscrossing there, and the Scruggs Vandervort and Barney department store busy with all its shoppers, though to tell the truth, in these hard times, more lookers than shoppers. So it's the last place in the entire world you would have expected something like this to happen. Broad daylight, June 28, summer sun already hot enough to marshmallow the street tar, fans whirling in the Cardinals' dugout pushing the steamy air from one end to the other.

I was sitting in our Ford in a blind alleyway where my father had parked it, across the way from J & J Jewelers. He had a three o'clock appointment to show his samples of Bulova watches that were in a large leather case with wheels that he could pull. He had me in the Ford to watch out for the repleviners in case they showed up. It was my father's constant worry, wherever we went, to keep tabs on the repleviners who, he said, were two guys from the finance company who had a court paper called a replevin that allowed them to snatch our Ford because my father had not made the regular payments for many months. The truth is my father couldn't pay anyone anything, including the electric company, the gas company, and landlords, saying that "in a Depression as bad as this, everyone should hold their horses." When I asked him how I'd recognize these repleviners he said I couldn't miss them, one big and fat with a walrus mustache, the other tall and skinny, both wearing black suits and derbies. If I spotted them I was to sound the horn four quick times, he would come lickety-splitting across Olive and speed the Ford away while I was to go across Olive and get the Bulova case. I didn't think the jewelry people would hand the case to some twelve-year-old kid, but I didn't say anything to my father because I thought the repleviners would not be way downtown on Olive looking for this rickety Ford. My father had been on this replevin lookout for many months now.

"Another thing, no matter what," my father had warned me, "two streetcars collide, Scruggs Vandervort burns up, you don't leave Bertha. Without her I can't cover customers on my

Bulova list and I will be back trying to sell those god-awful glass candlesticks."

He was talking about the hollow glass candlesticks filled with colored threads, with red threads coming out of the top like pretend flames. He used to go door to door trying to sell those dumb candlesticks, but with everyone Depression-busted they were not in the mood for fake candlesticks or actually they weren't in the mood to buy watches either. But he did get twenty-five dollars every week from the Bulova Company and that paid some of the charge for my mother's keep at the Fee-Fee Sanitarium in Creve Coeur plus bought us a little food but not enough to pay even part of the rent. He'd only had this Bulova job since March, and he was very anxious to make some sales so he could keep it. Most of the watches were just cases with no insides, but all lined up in rows inside the sample case they were something beautiful to look at.

Sitting in the Ford, broiling in the afternoon sun, I watched my father pull his sample case across Olive to the J & J door where he pushed the button that would buzz him in. As he started to open the buzzing door a fat man with a beard wearing overalls and a sloppy tennis hat, the rim down around his face, standing on the sidewalk, quick got in behind my father and followed him into the store before the door closed. Right away I felt funny, the way I get when I feel bad news is coming, like the doctor listening all over my mother's back with his listener in his ears and I know before he says it that Mom had to go to the sanitarium. The way that fat man got in back of my father gave me that feeling. I strained my eyes to watch the J & J door, hoping to see my father come out pulling his sample case but it didn't happen. What did happen was the boom, boom of gunshots, the big glass window with "J & J Jewelers" on it shattering to pieces, the door flying open, the fat man in the floppy cap coming out with a bag in one hand and a gun in the other that he was putting in his pocket as he walked down the street and disappeared among the Scruggs Vandervort and Barney people.

With the door open now, I saw my father with his sample case coming toward the door but before he could make it out the traffic cop came running with his gun in his hand and pushed him back in. I thought maybe I should go over and try to help him, but as I started to roll up the windows and lock the Ford, two more cops showed up in a cop car and the sidewalks flooded with onlookers. The sound of sirens screaming like swords cutting the air was getting closer and closer, piercing my head. I was on my knees behind the windshield to see what was happening, numb, unable to move or clear up my head, the crowd being pushed back from the jewelry store by the cops. Two cops on long-legged horses who had been on patrol were now forcing their horses through the crowd making a way for a sireny ambulance to get to the store. A cop who had been guarding the door now opened it as two men from the ambulance hurried in, pushing a stretcher on wheels.

I tried to see inside as the door opened, hoping to glimpse my father, but the door quickly closed and in no time it opened again and the ambulance men came out pushing the stretcher, this time with a man on it covered with a sheet. People in the crowd jostled each other, trying to get close to the stretcher for a good look, the horse cops having to push them out of the way so the stretcher could get back inside the ambulance. It took off as soon as the door closed, its siren back to screaming, pushing its way through the stubborn crowd. From where I was I couldn't tell if the man on the stretcher covered with a sheet was dead or alive.

Happening 2

The worst was yet to come.

The door opened and there was my father coming out, the sight of him making me feel good but only for a second because instead of his sample case behind him, there were the two cops who had come in their cop car. That's when my heart stopped. Instead of pulling the sample case, my father's arms were bent in back of him and on his wrists were handcuffs. Handcuffs! But why? What was going on? He didn't shoot that man. The fat man did. I should run over and tell those cops what I saw. The fat man sneaking in. The fat man putting a gun in his pocket.

But before I could move, one cop opened the back door of his car, my father got in, the cop closed the door and got in the front seat beside his partner who drove away, no siren, and whoof!, my father was gone. To jail, I guess.

I sat there dumbed out, my brain scrambled, no one to turn to, afraid. I felt crying coming up but I am not a crier and I tried hard to put it down. I was roasting in the Ford's furnace that was getting stoked by the St. Louis sun.

I pushed myself to open all the windows but the air that came in was harder to breathe than the air inside. The rubberneckers had thinned out a little now that the ambulance had disappeared with the guy under the sheet. But there were cop cars and cops hanging around the J & J store, which meant that things were still on the skillet so I better figure out pretty quick just what I should do. Our life had given me some preparation for that. I had gone to eleven different grammar schools because my father had signed all those Depression leases—the ones where landlords gave two or three months of free rent. We'd pack up the night before the free rent ran out and move to a new place that offered a whole new period of free rent. Landlords were all in terrible shape because of a glut of vacant flats. I did all right in the new schools because one thing I am is a whiz at writing and when the new teachers saw the sentences this new kid could string together their eyes would light up and sometimes they would even advance me a grade.

But my best experience was last summer

when we were all living in one room in the Westgate Hotel on Kingshighway and Delmar. That was the time that the doctor at the clinic sent my mother to the Fee-Fee Sanitarium to treat her lungs for consumption, which is what they called it. It was also the time my father got a watch-strap line to sell what he called "on the road," the road being Illinois and Iowa. I didn't think watch straps would light up a lot of buyers but they did give my father a break from the glass candles that he kept under one of our beds. Of course my father going on the road meant I would be living alone in 303. He arranged for me to have meals with Mr. Dinapoulus downstairs at the Dew Drop Inn. "You're the man of the house now, Aaron," my father said as he gave me two silver dollars "for any emergencies."

I think I would have been all right if that eviction notice hadn't been glued to our door. Several rooms besides ours also got them. "For nonpayment of rent now seriously in arrears, you are to vacate your premises immediately without removing any of your possessions which will remain with the Westgate until your debt has been satisfied." But I knew that as long as

I stayed in our room the landlord, Mound City Savings Bank, could not send Doug, the disgusting, bloodthirsty bellboy, into our room to do his dirty work.

But I had one big problem—I could not leave the room to go down to the Dew Drop Inn on the corner to get something to eat. I could fill up on only so much water. Also the hotel had shut off our room's electricity so forget about reading after dark even if I had some library books I wanted to read. The Atwater Kent's tubes had long ago burned out. The only good thing was the taxi dance hall in the basement of the hotel, the Good Times. On a good night, when it carried up, I could listen to the music played by the band: saxophone, piano, and drums. During the night, Doug, the rat-faced bellboy, would scratch on the door and make spooky noises. To defend myself, like I sometimes saw in the movies, I pushed the dresser and the two chairs and the linoleum-top table against the door. But what I couldn't do anything about was that I was starting to starve. I finally got so hungry, so out-of-my-mind hungry, that I ate the full-color picture of a roast beef that was in an old copy of a *Woman's Home Companion* that I found on the floor of the closet. I scissored the roast beef nicely, salted it, and I swear every mouthful tasted like eating the real thing. I even ate the little round potatoes that were in the picture with it.

I washed it all down with glasses of water and felt much, much better, but later that night I woke up with a killer stomachache.

Just about that time a note was slipped under the door, brought by someone on behalf of my father. He was back and suggested I pile on all the clothes I had, which wasn't much, and told me where to meet him.

I did, leaving the remainder of the busted and unusable stuff, like torn umbrellas, in the room, thinking I would never have to go through anything like that again, but now here I was, only difference I was alone in a big city with my pop in trouble with the cops. He had obviously not told them about me roasting in the Ford or they certainly would have come across Olive by now to get me.

The Ford and me were sitting ducks. I had practiced starting it and shifting it but my legs weren't long enough to reach the clutch and brake pedals so there was no way I could get it out of the alley, and sooner or later the Ford and me would wind up like all sitting ducks.

My head was stuffed with worries:

(One) Why had they taken my father away in handcuffs and where was he?

(Two) The Bulova case loaded with its watches was in the jewelry store with no one to keep an eye on it.

(Three) I have forty-seven cents in my pocket, total, but I have three quarters secretly hidden in a Fatima cigarette tin back at our place at the Tremont but how do I get at it? We had two rooms, one with a bed, the other with a Murphy In-A-Dor, which is where I slept. I also had my All-City Transportation Pass that they forgot to pick up when school closed for the summer. An eagle-eyed bus or streetcar conductor might grab it, but then again I'm pretty good at the quick way I flash it.

My number A-one worry was that someone might tell my mother about my father and his handcuffs. Being upset was considered very bad for consumption and my poor mother was an outstanding worrier.

I thought of one more thing that needed one hundred percent attention: me. With my mother in a strict sanitarium and my father probably in jail, it was the city's duty to take charge of me, like putting me in one of the city's orphanages.

Of course, if that happened I would not be able to help anyone. It almost did happen to me when I was guarding our room at the Westgate and a woman with a badge from welfare came looking for me, but I hid in the closet hanging on the inside of my father's old raincoat, scrunching up my legs.

My mind snapped back to the present when a shiny new four-door Studebaker pulled up to the store, the driver's door flinging open and a large important-looking man got out, slammed the door, pushed a path through the people in his way, barked something at the cop in front of the store, and was quickly let in. Maybe someone who could help my father. That got me going. I rolled up the windows, drank the last of the water in my thermos, locked the doors, crossed my fingers, and headed across Olive.

Happening 3

The sidewalk in front of the store had been blocked off and there were hunks of glass all over the place. I picked my way through the crowd that still clogged the street, feeling lost and unsure what my next move should be or could be. One of the horse cops pushed his way in to me and squashed me up against a tall man who was standing at the barricade writing something on a pad. He had a card tucked under the brim of his hat that said PRESS POST-DISPATCH. Maybe I could find out something from him. I pulled on his seersucker to get his attention but with all the horse-shoving he paid no attention to me.

The store door opened and a beefy man in a black suit with a diamond stickpin on his tie and a badge on a chain around his neck came out and the *Post-Dispatch* man said, "Hello, Lieutenant. Jack Carmen of the *Dispatch*."

"How's it hanging, Jack?" the lieutenant said.

"Not too wobbly," the reporter said. "Whatcha got for me?"

"To quote?"

"Yes, sir."

"It's Fitsgibbons with an *s*, forget the *z*, okay?"

"You bet. It's the copy desk screwed up. Who was the stiff they wheeled outa here?"

"One of the salespeople—Dempsey by name. His shot hit the front window and the perp's hit Dempsey's right eye, a bull's-eye, all right."

"Dempsey fired first?"

"Yup. The perp had his gun out for show while he scooped up the swag—"

"Was that one of the J brothers just arrived?"

"Crusty bastard."

"Did he have any—"

"Nothing to tell me except letting me know that he was aces at city hall and we better catch the shooter who did this or heads will fall, mine included."

"How about the guy hustled outa here in handcuffs?"

"Watch salesman—or so he says. The perp came in on his tail. Foreigner. They'll keep him overnight and try to hold him as a material."

"Courtroom four?"

"Yup."

A black Lincoln driven by a uniformed cop, St. Louis police logo on its door, drove up and the lieutenant got in.

"Thanks, Lieutenant," Jack said.

"Remember about the *s*," the lieutenant said through the window as the Lincoln pulled away.

I tugged on his seersucker and the reporter looked down at me. "Where is courtroom four?"

"Criminal Courts Building," he said as he put his notebook in his pocket and started to go.

I gave his jacket another tug. "What's a material?"

He kept going, in a hurry. I guess to tell the *Post-Dispatch* what the lieutenant had just told him.

ME BEING right there in front of the J & J store, I thought about the Bulova case on the other side of the door. Maybe the door cop would let me in to explain who I was and how I would take care of the case, but then again without the Ford how would I take the sample case anywhere. And on top of that I would have to deal with Mr. Jankman and hearing how crusty he'd been with a police lieutenant, I could imagine how snotty he'd be with a scruffy twelve-year-old kid, so I chickened out and got on an Olive streetcar heading uptown.

≡

Happening 2

≡

When I got to the door of our apartment, 12B, I came smack up against an official police notice tacked on the door:

TAKE NOTICE
City of St. Louis
Premises under police control
until further notice
13th Precinct

I tried my key in the door. Sure enough, didn't work. My heart sunk pretty bad. The two rooms, bathroom, kitchen, and In-A-Dor of 12B was a godsend jump up from the shabby one-room 303 of the Westgate Hotel, no kitchen, toilet down at the end of the hall, but now I was worse off than at the Westgate since I had no parents and nowhere to go for the night. Although I couldn't think my way into some place I might bed down, I did think of someone who might be able to help me out with the Ford, if it was still there in the alley—Vernon, the super who lived in a basement room at the Tremont. Also, he might have been there when the cops came to lock us out of 12B. Anyway he was always very nice to me and I often hung out with him when I came home from school and mom was in the sanitarium and my father was out peddling whatever he was out peddling. One day I came home from school with my face banged up from being knocked around by Tony Razzolo, a big bully who somehow had it in for me. Maybe because I was at the top of my class and he was at the bottom. That particular time I came home with my face swolled up and my lip bloody, Vernon had me come into his place and he washed my face with a cloth dipped in alcohol which hurt so much tears popped out of my eyes.

When he was much younger Vernon had been a prizefighter and there were pictures all over the walls of his super-neat room of him in prizefighting poses. He said if I wanted he would give me a lesson on how to not get beat up.

"But he's way bigger 'n me and his hands are the size of tennis rackets."

"Big don't matter if you can't land with 'em. I'm gonna teach you how to make 'em miss."

And he sure did. He'd have an after-school snack ready, piece of corn bread, say, and then he'd put on those old cracked boxing gloves of his.

"Most everyone don't know fiddly-poop about prizefighting and they aim all their punches at the other guy's jaw, big roundhouse wallops, but no matter how big he is and strong as Herkalees it don't do him no good 'less it lands and it won't hit nothin' long as what he's aimin' at keeps movin'. So that's what you're g'wanta do. Bad guy comes at you, fists all doubled up, you's bobbin' your head this way and that, feet doin' a little shuffle, left, right, in, out, all of you movin' this way and that, no matter what part'a you he thros at you're not receivin' it, and I guarantee you this, all his haymaker punches whistling thoo the air and hittin' nothin' wear him down faster'n him runnin' ten times round the track. So that's what we're gonna practice. If your head had been swivlin' and your feet doin' the heeby-jeeby shuffle, that there Tony would've landed nothin'.'"

Vernon was a very good teacher and it didn't take me long to pick up the swivel and the shuffle, and the next time Tony started to pick on me to show off in front of pretty Edna Coyle he was trying to impress, I stood up to his insults, gave as good as I got, and he came at me with his fists ready, my head-swivels and quick heeby-jeebies made him miss and every time he missed I juked to the side and hit him in the breadbasket and that made him holler and double over and give up on fighting.

After that he never once bothered me again. In fact, Edna Coyle walked with me between classes and didn't give Tony the time of day.

EVEN THOUGH there were scars on Vernon's face from when he was a prizefighter—the scars sort of stood out lighter than his dark skin—and one of his ears was kind of squished, he had a wonderful smile and he laughed a lot and that made him nice to look at. It also helped that he seemed to like everyone and everyone liked him.

I went down the steps and knocked on his door. I was glad to hear radio music, which meant he was there.

"Hello, lad, come right on in." He mostly called me lad or sonny boy. "I been aspecting you. Sit you down over there and tell me what your daddy done that got the po-lice here, pokin' all over your 'partment and lock you out."

I told him how the day went and how the cops

arrested my father and how the case of watches was left in the jewelry store and how the Ford had to be rescued from the alley though it might not be there anymore.

"I was wondering, Vernon," I said, "if you would go down to Olive with me to where Scruggs is and drive it out of that alley before the pleviners find it."

"I sure would but truth is I don't know how to drive an automobile . . . let me think . . . yep, my cousin Arthur do—he used to drive Peverly Dairy afore they laid him off 'cause the 'Pression. Don't know if'n he still has a phone—we ain't communercated for a spell, but I'll try him out."

He went to his telephone and dialed a number. His face lit up when he got an answer.

"Hey, Pickles, it's the big V, happy I can still get your ear. How come you able 'ford a telephone? . . . Oh, once a week? You and Maybelle able to get by all right? . . . Oh, I'm okay—Tremont chizzled me down some 'cause we got lots of vacancies plus lots no pays 'n slow pays but Tiger 'n me stretches it out."

Tiger was an old collie and something else. "Listen, Pickles, got a favor to ask. Lad here from 12B they got some trouble needs his papa's Ford picked up down on Olive across Scruggs before the finance get it, would you go drive it for him? Pay you back the car fare . . . To where? . . . Well, any place be safe for a spell. Damn nice o' you, Pickles. I'll be owin' you one. Meet you front of Scruggs."

I thanked Vernon and hoped this might be the one good thing happening that day.

"We best get goin'," Vernon said as he reached for the old cap he always wore, but then he interrupted himself. "You hungry, lad? When's the last time you had somethin' to eat?"

"There was a bag of pretzels in the Ford."

"In other words, you's hungry."

"Oh, not to worry," I told him. "I'm not used to eating regular. What's important's rescuing the Ford."

Vernon had taken a covered dish from an overhead shelf. "Made this sweet potato pie this mornin'," he said. He cut a large slice for me. It looked wonderful and made me realize how hungry I was. I took it with thanks. Said I'd eat it on the way and we started out the door to catch the number nine streetcar. It was a wonder he could cook up a dish as good as that from his old beat-up smoky stove.

Happening 5

The sidewalk was busy since Scruggs stayed open till nine Thursday nights. Vernon said that cousin Arthur tended to be on the small side and that it might not be easy spotting him. The busted window at J & J Jewelers had been boarded up and the two cops who stood on guard kept rubberneckers moving.

Cousin Arthur showed up and gave Vernon a friendly wallop on his arm followed by a hug around his waist, which was about as far up as he could get since, as Vernon had said, Arthur tended small and Vernon tended very large. Arthur and I said howdy-do and shook hands, mine with some remains of sweet potato pie on it.

"Just where's this Ford?" Arthur asked.

I pointed to the alley.

"Right smack across from the cops," Vernon said with a shake of his head.

"Yeah," Arthur said. "Two black gents lookin' like us revin' up a Ford at night might throw a little suspicion their way."

"Oh, I'll vouch for you—not to worry."

"They want to see papers—you got papers?"

"What kind of papers?"

"Like who the owner?"

"My father has all that."

"So they ask where your papa and you say in jail because he was in that jewelry store today when that man got killed," Vernon said, shaking his head again.

"And I be the one with my hands on the wheel," Arthur said.

"Okay, listen," I said, "tell you what." I handed the key to Arthur. "You and Vernon go get in the Ford and while you start it up I'll be across the street getting the cops' attention. You'll drive to the back of Scruggs where the trucks make deliveries and I'll catch up with you there."

"How you gonna deal with them cops?"

"Don't know yet but I'll think of something."

Arthur looked at the key in his hand, not convinced.

Vernon said, "Arthur's been in and out the clink a lot. What's it been, Pickles? Four times?"

"Five. First when we was in Little Rock.

Wasn't nothin' but vittles for Maybelle and the kids."

"And the Jack Daniel's?"

"That needy medicine for me."

I started across the street, my brain busy on how I'm going to get the cops looking at me and not at the Ford poking its bent nose out of the alley. I was stepping up on the sidewalk when a man came running my way, a woman running after him yelling, "Stop him! Thief! My bag! My bag! Thief! Thief!" As the man came running by me I did what any red-blooded American boy would do—I stuck out my foot and the man tangled with my Ked and went zippety-kerplop, the purloined bag skidding into the gutter. (I learned that swell word "purloined" from Mr. Edgar Allan Poe, of whom I am a colossal fan, along with Mr. Jules Verne, Mr. Mark Twain, Mr. Guy de Maupassant, Mr. Charles Dickens to name a few.)

As the two cops were busy pulling the thief out of the gutter, I saw the Ford coming onto Olive, headed toward the back of Scruggs. All full of thanks, the lady got hold of her bag, but when one of the cops said to the other, go get the kid's name, I thought that would be a good time to go hook up with Bertha.

———

"SO, LAD, where you plan spend the night?" Vernon asked. We were sitting in the back of the Ford.

"Haven't had time to think about that," I said to him.

"Thought you said he lived at the Tremont?" Arthur said from behind the wheel.

"Yeah, he do, but the po-lice lock it up and 'sides there was a woman come around lookin' for him . . ." He started to fish an old stuffed-up billfold out of his pocket.

"You must have a lot of valuables to own a fancy wallet like that," I said.

"Mrs. Van Hurst, 9B, give it to me when her hubby passed . . . oh, here it is." He pulled out a card. "Freda Muller, Juvenile Welfare, telephone number to call when you showed up. Said important I call her. Mean looker. Dressed all in black, top to bottom."

"No, you don't," I said. "They stash me in one of those juvenile dumps, how I'm going to see about my father getting out?"

"I could let you bed down in one of our vacants—God knows we got enough o' them—

but the owner, Mr. Birdswell, who's tighter'n a cheap collar, always preachin' no pay, no stay. He find you freebee in one a his furnished vacants, he skin your rabbit ass."

"How about you got a relative or some friend?" Arthur said. "I can drop you off."

My mother's family did live in St. Louis until my grandfather, a short Hungarian with a bristly mustache and an even bristlier personality, burned down his restaurant for the insurance, but the cheapie arson guy botched the job and burned down the entire block of stores, and Grandpa, Grandma (who did the cooking), and my mother's two sisters got out of St. Louis just before the police came looking for them.

We had no other relatives and the Depression got rid of the few friends we did have. What with all that had been happening I hadn't had time to think about what to do now that I was homeless.

"They's a city place on Cherokee got homeless beds," Arthur said, reading my mind.

"They only take kids who're with they's parents, dummy," Vernon said. " 'Sides he check in there this Freda woman gonna nab him. She got the looks o' someone you don't want lookin' for you."

We were on Lindell going alongside Forest Park. I told Arthur to pull over, that the park was as good a place as any to spend the night.

"You watch out," Vernon said. "I hear they's gangs steal things while you sleepin'."

"Like what?"

"Food, clothes, shoes—"

"These busted Keds?" I held up my right foot. The broken laces were double-knotted and the Keds marker was hanging half off. "Welcome to them."

I got out of the Ford, spoke to Arthur through the driver's window, asked him where he was going to hide the Ford.

"Friend a mine's got a used-parts place," he said. "There's a whole mountain of tires, hide it behind 'em."

"What about at night when no one's there? Is it safe?"

"Well, he got chain link, barb wire, and three Rottweilers," he said, putting the Ford in first and taking off.

Happening 6

Forest Park was my second home, or maybe I should say my first because when you've lived all of you in a one-room scruffy place like we did at the Westgate, that smells old and sour—well, the park with its tennis courts, ball fields, basketball hoops, art museum, Muny opera, terrific zoo, fountains, all that stuff is pretty much like rescuing you from drowning. So it was only natural to think about the good ol' park, but what I did not have in mind for sleeping was the hard slats of a park bench where someone could steal off you. No, what I did have in mind were the tennis courts where I knew there was an open shed where old nets, brooms, liners, and such were stored. All the valuable stuff like rackets, balls, visors, sweatbands, etcetera were kept in the main place that was locked at night.

One more important thing about me and the shed, it taught me how to play tennis. Really. The wall at the back of the shed had a white line painted across it, exactly the height of the tennis net on the court. And that is where hour after hour, day after day I would hit an old tennis ball that would come bouncing back to me. My style was not as classy as the kids who could afford lessons, but I would beat them in twelve-and-under tournaments.

The other thing makes me give credit to the wall was throwing a baseball. Not the real leather baseball that wouldn't bounce back, but the practice kind of hard rubber, exact same size, given to me by Mr. Plagg, the baseball coach at Kennard, the grammar school I just graduated from now that I'm about to start junior high. He said I had "potential" and that for my age I threw a nice little curve, which almost no kids my age are able to do.

As I started to make myself some kind of bed to sleep on, I was thinking of Mr. Plagg who wasn't at the school anymore because there wasn't any money for his salary. In fact, not for any baseball at all. Or basketball. Or track. Or football. Or field hockey, which was a girl thing that I don't really care about.

I folded a tennis net and covered it with a smooth piece of tarp, put it on top of a pile of old nets, and made a pillow out of an old tennis jacket that hung on a broom handle. I opened the window next to the pile of nets and let the moon shine through. I climbed up the mound of nets and found a good level spot to lie on. It wasn't anything like my Murphy bed but it felt good to stretch out.

My mind got to thinking about my father and where he might be. Jail, no doubt, but what kind? All the movies I'd seen that had jails had cramped, dumpy upper-downers, where the good guys had to climb the uppers while mean-looking desperadoes were on the lowers. The jail food was fed to them like I'd seen animals fed at the Forest Park zoo, only the animal food looked a whole lot better than the jail crud.

My father, who I sometimes call Pop but mostly Father, was not your regular American dad. He was lots older than my mom who was eighteen and he was thirty-three when they got married. My mom told me she had gone to secretary school to learn typing and a funny kind of writing called shorthand so she could get a job and free herself from her terrible father, my grandfather (she didn't call him "terrible," that's my word). She got a job at eighteen dollars a week, gave most of it to my grandma, but that wasn't enough for my grandfather who was after her for all of it and threatened her with his awful black belt. She never gave in, not my mom. So I'm sure she was anxious to get out of that house and that was one of the reasons she said yes to my father. Another reason, I guess, was he lived a steady life and owned a fur store. My mother told me all this, not my father who almost never said anything much about his early life, not even about the place where he was born or where he went to school.

All I knew was that a relative who had come from Poland had started a fur shop in St. Louis and brought my father over as a young man to join his family and work in the store. After many years the relative said he had decided to go back to Poland with his family and he turned the business over to my father. So when he married my mother that was the fur shop that he owned. I was born two years later.

My earliest remembrance is living in a very nice apartment on Art Hill Place and that there was a nanny named Mildred who wore a white dress and always had a flower in her hair. She liked to sing and taught me songs that we often sang together. One Christmas we performed a dance she made up and we danced for my mother and father to the music on the Victrola and they clapped happily and Mildred took my hand and we made a nice little bow.

It was that Christmas that my father gave me my first suit and Mildred a beautiful hat with colored ribbons and tiny birds. After dinner, in front of the tree, he gave my mom a jewelry box tied with a gold ribbon that contained a ring that had a large shiny brown diamond with little white diamonds around it. My mother cried out a happy cry and put it on her finger and kissed my father on his lips which I had never seen her do before, only cheeks.

It was all right to have a new suit, but, honestly, I had hoped it would be a Lou Gehrig baseball mitt or a Bill Tilden tennis racket, but coming from Europe, the only sport my father could relate to was soccer, and there was not much of that. He was a proper man. He wore very nice suits made for him by what he called "Old World tailors" and he wore a proper tie with a fine stickpin every day, even at Sunday breakfast. The stickpin was the only thing that really impressed me. It was a solid-gold head and shoulders of an

African prince with a high turban of pearls and beautiful diamonds for his eyes. Seeing that gold stickpin in the fold of one of his elegant silk ties made all the dark days to come a little bit better. And days it had to be put in the pawnshop made a dark day darker. That's where it was now, in Nathan's on DeBaliviere with its three gold balls hanging over the front door. And certainly you couldn't have a day darker than this one.

I WOKE UP in the night from a horrible dream of lions attacking me, red lions dripping blood. I was throwing baseballs at them, pitching at their snarling mouths, but I was losing the fight when waking up saved me. It took a while to get myself together and recognize where I was and what was happening. There was a busy, scratchy sound in the pile of nets beneath me that I recognized because there had been mice in our room at the Westgate. One of them, I called it Mickey, often ran around the molding on the ceiling.

I sat up in front of the open window hoping for good air but the air coming in was just as hot and heavy. The moon had moved on. I climbed down from my sleep perch and went outside to pee on the grass. I didn't have a wristwatch but there were smudges of light starting to appear in the black sky and I figured June daylight was not far off. I went to a nearby court and climbed up the referee's stand and sat me down in the high chair.

Happening 7

In a couple of hours, I would be going from this clay court to the criminal court where they would bring my father, maybe in handcuffs; the thought of having to be on my own among all those court people with their uniforms and robes and badges and guns made my stomach flip-flop. What will I do when my father approaches? Go over to him? Wave to him? Send him a note? Pretend not to know him? Will he wave to me? Or will he look at me, pretending not to know me, letting me know I should do likewise?

About my father and me, it's true we didn't have many things we did together. Like going to ball games. He tried but he could not figure out the whole craziness (to him) of balls and strikes, hits, double plays, walks, steals, and all the rest. I tried to teach him how to throw and catch a baseball so we could have catches, but it didn't work. No matter how much I tried he continued to throw like a girl, and he poked at the ball with his glove instead of letting it come to him and catching it in the pocket.

But even though we didn't do many things together, my father was a big fan of mine. He carried my report cards around and proudly showed off the As and Bs and what the teachers wrote about my English, writing, and athletic leadership which I guess was being captain of the baseball team. He came to all my events with my mother and was a big clapper for me at oratorical contests and when I acted in plays. Over the top when I was a winner and mad at the judges and umpires when I wasn't. Really proud of me.

A very good family life we had, until the doom of the Night and Day. That one thing, that one terrible thing and all we were, our whole life, fell apart without warning, out of the blue, the Night and Day Bank, one of the biggest banks in St. Louis, locked its doors, turned out the lights, and put up a sign:

CLOSED

My father had everything he had, every penny, in that one bank. So did I. Twenty-two dollars, saved up in my own savings account, little by little. My father had no backup. No company or person he could borrow from. His relations in Europe had hard times too. Everything all around him was caving in. The Night and Day sent a letter that said it would pay a penny for every dollar but they never even paid that. My father sold all his furs to other stores to pay off some of what he owed but it wasn't enough to even get even. He had to let Mildred go (she and I had a good cry) and he told our landlord we were leaving the apartment. We sold all the good stuff and that kept us going for a while.

My father tried to get a job with one of the fur shops he knew but they were all firing employees or going out of business themselves. My father sold our Buick but not for very much because everyone was selling their cars and no one was buying. Some of the kids in my class whose pops had certain jobs like doctors and cops, politicians and conductors, still brought hefty lunches, but the really rich kids and the medium kids like me had lunches that got skinnier and skinnier and often no lunches at all. But the worst was when a couple of kids who had dads who were really rich big shots were absent because their dads, like mine, had lost everything, but not able to face it, like mine, had killed themselves. Jumped out of the high-up windows where the big companies were on Pine Street. One of the kids was my good pal Benjamin who was the catcher on our baseball team when I was the pitcher. With him gone, Billy Joe, our second baseman, had to switch to catching but though he had a face mask and a chest protector he ducked every time the batter swung, so thanks to Billy Joe I lost my first game of the season. Didn't really matter because the principal, Mr. Stellwagon, canceled baseball "for economic reasons," he said in the notice he sent to every classroom.

IT WAS light enough now for a few of the earliest tennis birds to start arriving. A pair of ancient ones wearing sweat-stained sun visors, floppy shorts, T-shirts featuring Listerine, and clay-crusted tennis shoes came on my court and began volleying with an ancient tennis ball that was as gray and bald as they were.

I climbed down from the umpire's chair and went over to the water fountain. The courts were filling up. That's how it was now—play before eight and you don't have to pay or have a permit, but I had worked out a deal with Buddy Silverstone, who was in charge, for sweeping the courts in exchange for free play time. He also saved cracked rackets for me that could be fixed good enough to play. As for balls, court fifteen had an outside drain that could swallow a ball hit over the fence and make it disappear, but not if you knew where the drain ended.

The snack place, the Drop Shot, was starting up and coffee was in the air reminding me that I was hungry. Not for coffee, I don't drink coffee, but my mom always fixed me a pretty good breakfast, even if we were in the Westgate or one of those others that didn't allow food in the rooms. But a glass of milk and a slice of bread with margarine or peanut butter was about the best I could do with her in the sanitarium. I still had the forty-seven cents in my pocket but I figured the day being what it would be I'd better hang on to it. Thinking about my mom and breakfast I could hear the arguments she had with my father those times we had nothing for breakfast.

"Fred," she would say, "it's not right we send Aaron to school on an empty stomach."

"Maybe Piggly Wiggly will give us a little credit. I'll have a talk with Dave."

"You know what he said last week—absolutely positively not."

"I know. I know. But what do you want me to do, Ina? There is nothing left to sell. I took the steamer trunk to three places."

"What about the brown diamond?"

"You know it's at Nathan's."

"Yes but it's time to sell it. Nathan already told you."

"Now, Ina, don't start up!" My father thumped his hands on the table and raised his voice. He turned to me. "Aaron, why don't you go out and play."

Standing there outside the door I'd hear my mother say something about how the brown diamond would help us out for months to come.

My father would say not as much as you think since it has a flaw and wouldn't get nearly as much as one that didn't.

"But it would get enough so we could get by when we run out, wouldn't it?"

They would argue back and forth, but the last time I heard this, my father suddenly stopped arguing and said for my mom to give him her hand and sit beside him. His voice got soft and he spoke in a teary way, saying that the brown diamond for him was the last thing that stayed in their lives. That it reminded him of the business that was such a success and reminded him of how much he loved her the Christmas Day he gave it to her and reminded him of how pretty she was with joy on her face standing there in front of the tree with the lights on her as she turned the brown diamond this way and that and kissed him with much love and happiness. "Someday, somehow, I'll get it back from Nathan who said he'd hold it for me, and we will again be loving as we were."

"Hey, Aaron," Buddy called out, breaking in on my remembering. He was standing at the wide-open space on the side of his place where he delivered his orders. "How about a doughnut? You look like you need a sugar doughnut. My treat." I guess I did look kind of poopy. I took a big delicious bite and it made me hope it was going to be a day as spiffy as the doughnut.

Happening 8

Courtroom four was on the second floor of the Criminal Courts Building and it was packed when I got there. Not only was I feeling panicked by all the people and activity but also by a sign outside the door of the courtroom: "Children under 16 not admitted unless accompanied by an adult." I was big for my age but nowhere near looking sixteen. So the first thing I had to do was hook up with an adult. I watched everyone as they came up the stairs, feeling pretty hopeless, until an elderly gentleman who seemed alone came off the top step. His clothes were old but proper, his bow tie rather ragged but his beard and mustache nicely trimmed.

As he headed toward the courtroom I walked close beside him and the door cop let us pass.

"Sir," I said, acting as needy as I could, "could I please sit beside you?" I blurted out why I was there and he seemed pleased to help me. He explained that he was retired and that these daily court sessions were his best way to pass time. He explained that everyone who had been arrested and put in an overnight holding cell, like my father, had families and friends and lawyers and people called bailsmen who I never heard of who were all there. The many policemen, he explained, were connected to the arrests of those jailed and would report to the judge. He offered me a box of mints that he opened and I gladly took one, in fact two.

Suddenly, in a loud voice, the uniform at the head of the courtroom said that everyone should rise and come to order and the room did. A judge came in, sat behind the desk, and there followed a parade of the locked-ups, arrested for all kinds of things: hitting a wife, not paying parking tickets, hit-and-run, alimony, peeing in the street, driving with no license, on and on, all wrapped up with lawyers and bailsmen and cops and suddenly there was my father, a cop taking him in front of the judge.

"Frederick Broom, Your Honor, material witness in FM23W5, the J & J Jewelry murder case."

The judge was looking at the papers he'd been given. "Naturalized?"

"Foreign accent. Entered with the killer. Held

jewelry bag for him. Prior arrest for jumping electricity."

I gasped when I heard that about jumping the electricity. He'd take the electric line out of the meter box and twist it direct onto the other end of the line. Very dangerous because he could get electrocuted but he only had to go to jail once but not for very long, maybe a day or so because so many people were getting locked up for doing the same thing and the jails were spilling over. But now the judge was looking at him like he killed a dozen people.

My father started to say something but the judge stopped him, said he'd get his chance to talk at the trial. Meanwhile, he would be confined until trial. "Next."

My father again tried to say something but the cop pushed him away. As my father turned, he looked straight at me, smiled, and slightly shook his head left-right meaning "no." I started to get up to go down the aisle between the benches to try to talk to him but the cop had him gone before I could get out of my seat. I was close to tears and hurt and befuddled (which was a favorite word of mine) but I put my head down for a minute and remembered that I had a new friend next to me.

"He's a handsome man, your father," my new friend said. "As a material witness they can hold him without charges until the trial. You should try to get a lawyer."

"Lawyers cost a lot, don't they?" I said.

"Depends."

"I don't know anything about lawyers," I said. "Can you help me?"

"Oh, I wish but I'm not allowed."

I had no idea what he meant. "Not allowed?"

"Well, yes, I am not to have any contact with anyone who is, well, like you—a child."

"But I'm not really—"

"It's the numbers. Below twenty-one, and you're twelve."

It dawned on me. "And they busted you?"

"It hasn't been pretty. Now, sorry I am, but I have to terminate your company even though you're an admirable young man who needs help."

He got up, offered me another mint, and left. The locked-ups were still coming before the judge. I had no idea where to go, what to do, or how to go about it.

Happening 9

I left the courthouse and turned the corner onto Richmond, walking down the side of the street where the maple trees gave a little shade. My head was exploding with all kinds of things: finding a lawyer, somewhere to stay, somehow to eat, our apartment, the Bulova sample case, the Ford, my mother. The heat of the pavement was burning through the cracked soles of my busted Keds. The morning doughnut needed a refill.

At Fourth Street I came upon a church with open doors, Roman Catholic Church of the Immaculate Heart. The idea of sitting myself down in a quiet kind-of-cool church thinking things out was very appealing, but we were not church people although we own a Bible and I had studied the Bible, but we had no particular religion. We did Christmas, a tree and special eating when we could afford it, and sometimes I was invited to a church affair by one of my school friends, back in the days when things were okay and I had church-looking clothes, but I had never been in a Roman Catholic Church with priests waving incense and a choir singing or a synagogue where there was a special singer and chanting, all of which I had seen in the movies.

So it felt strange to go up the steps into the Immaculate Heart on my own. It was very nice and quiet and felt private. Only a few old people were in the pews praying. I sat myself down and looked around at the colored windows and saints and paintings of religious figures. I began to feel a little better, especially my feet.

Not far from me was a black standing box with a pointed roof and a black open curtain on one side of it that hung folded over a small window that was closed, with a chair up against the box under the window. There was a little red light shining on the pointed roof. The box had an open door that a heavy priest in his black robe was entering. He shut the door and the light on the roof turned from red to green. A woman who had been praying got up and went over to the box. She sat down on the chair, the little window opened, and she talked to the priest who had his ear at the window as she pulled across the black curtain in back of her, making her disappear. The green light now turned to red. I realized that I had seen these boxes in the movies and the priest was there to give advice to the people who told them about their problems and some bad things, sins they had committed. When the woman opened the curtain, she crossed herself and left the box. The red light turned green. I hadn't planned on it but just like that I found myself going to the box, getting on the chair to reach the little door, and tapping on the window. The priest slid open the screen and was surprised to see me.

"Excuse me, Father," I said, "I'm not a Catholic but is it okay to ask you about a problem I have—I mean, my family has, is that something that is okay with you?"

The priest was a large man with a hanging chin and a hearty laugh. His laugh ended with a heavy cough. "Unusual, yes, quite but go right ahead."

"I . . . we need a lawyer," I said, "and a Catholic one would be perfectly fine, thank you."

It took a while for the priest, who said to call him Father Tim, to figure out why I needed a lawyer. He knew all about the J & J killing so I guess priests don't spend all their time reading the Bible. He said he would look into the lawyer thing but in the meantime, with my father in jail, my mother in the sanitarium, and my apartment locked up, where was I staying? Like a dummy, without thinking, I told him the truth. Well, he said, that being so, nice young fella like me should have a proper place to stay and he would arrange for me to be taken by the Catholic Children's Center while he looked into the lawyer thing.

Saying that, he pushed open his door and with a heavy grunt pulled himself up and came out. I got down from my chair. Up close, he was wider and fuller.

"Come with me," he said, "I'll take you to Sister Ann, the Mother Superior, who runs the center."

I felt a river of panic run down my spine. "Oh, sir, Your Eminence, that's swell of you but if you don't mind I'd prefer not to get tied up since I have a whole lot of very important things to do."

As I was talking he was walking me to the back of the church and into a room where there were several nuns doing office things like typing and telephoning and writing in big bank-like books. One of the nuns who was sitting at her own desk that had a Mother Superior sign on it came over to Father Tim and greeted him. They went to the side of the room and had a private talk while I nearly died over getting myself into a dumb spot like this.

Father Tim finally came to me and said that Sister Ann would make a place for me while he would refer my situation to the deacon. He patted me on the head, said goodbye to the nuns, and waddled out of the room.

Sister Ann, who was a big woman with a big chin, said to come with her and she would get me settled in the center. The river down my back turned into a flood. She took me by the arm and opened the door. "It's just down the street," she said, leading me.

"Ma'am, Mother Superior," I said in a kind of panic, "do you mind, please, before I go, I have to pee." The sisters all gasped a little.

"The facility's just down the aisle," she said, pointing. "I'll take you to the door and wait."

"Oh, thanks, but you don't have to, I'll—"

"I will wait at the door," she said, chopping her words.

Of course I really didn't have to pee, but what I did have to do was get out of this and fast before Sister Ann got suspicious. It was a small room, one urinal, one sit-down toilet, a small sink with hot-cold handles, a paper-towel thing, and a little window with a screen that was pretty high up, way beyond my reach. The door of the sit-down toilet was closed, two shoes showing under the door, maybe someone who could help me reach the window. But, no, there was that heavy screen across it and besides it was too small to wiggle through even if somehow the screen busted open.

Even though I can easily fire up a way to get out of tough spots, either talk my way out or brain my way out, I was ready to admit I was stuck in the clutches of the Mother Superior and I would have to give in. I started for the door, accidently bumping over a basket that was full of used paper towels—that's when it hit me, remembering what happened that time we were living in that place on the roof of Sorkin's delicatessen and the bathroom water pipe broke and flooded the place.

I scooped up the paper towels and stuffed them into the drain in the sink, as I turned on both the hot and cold full blast. The water quickly started to flow over the top of the sink flooding the floor. I pushed the water, helping it run under the door. I called out for help. "We're flooding! We're flooding!" The water was hitting the shoes under the closed toilet door which now flew open as the occupant, his pants down, came barreling out and headed for the door which was just being opened by the Mother Superior, and the toilet man, hog-tied by his pants around his legs, crashed into the mother superior and they both got tangled up and landed on the watery floor. I carefully stepped around them and walked down the aisle to the front of the church. My Keds squished as I went down the steps of the cathedral onto the sidewalk, but in this heat I knew they would dry out in no time.

White Castle was having a two-burgers-and-a-soft-drink-for-five-cents one-day promo and I was at the counter of the White Castle on Jefferson getting my five cents' worth, leaving me with forty-two cents. After my close call with the Catholics, I decided it was dumb of me to try to get other people to find a lawyer, why not go get one myself? There was certainly enough of them all over the place, their names joined together with commas: Somebody, Somebody, and Somebody. Sometimes five somebodys. I planned to go to the Mercantile building and look them over on the board in the lobby.

I finished off my second White Castle, each burger thinner than a spiderweb but helped with free ketchup and mustard. I laced up my Keds that had dried out in the sun by now.

———

THERE WERE lots of three-, four-, and five-namers located in the Mercantile. Gary, Appleton and Bishop looked good to me, so I took the elevator to the twelfth floor and went to their office. Very high-class. Leather sofas and chairs. Even leather walls like I'd never seen before. Lady behind the desk said, "Yes?"

"I'd like to see Mr. Appleton, please." I liked the sound of his name.

"Does he expect you?"

"Well . . . no, but it's important."

The lady smiled at me, nice smile, and said Mr. Appleton only saw people by appointment. Perhaps my father should call and arrange one.

"That's just it," I said, "my father can't call and that's what I want to see Mr. Appleton about."

"Your father is not able to call? Why not?"

"He's in jail."

An inner door opened and two men came into the room, one saying to the other, thank you, Mr. Appleton. They shook hands and the man left. Mr. Appleton, a tall man with a trim mustache and a gold watch chain across his chest, looked at me and said, in a friendly way, "Who have we here?"

I told him my name and the desk lady told

him what I had told her. Mr. Appleton smiled, put his arm around me, and said, "Why, come right in, Mr. Broom, and let's talk."

It was a beautiful office with a full view of the Mississippi River. He sat down on a leather sofa next to me and a woman came in with two glasses of Coca-Cola on ice. I told him how my father came to be in jail as a material witness. He knew all about the J & J murder from reading about it in the *Post-Dispatch*. He asked me how old I was and said for my age I was certainly "far along."

"Tell you the truth, Aaron," he said, "as a material witness your dad hasn't been charged with a crime. He's just someone the prosecutor wants to hold until the trial. He may know something. So right now he can't get bail but even if he could that would be difficult and expensive. However, if they find the killer then the case would be closed and your father released, which is probably what is going to happen."

"So the important thing is to find the fat guy who fired the gun?"

"That's right but if they don't and there is a trial and your dad is still in trouble, you come see me and I'll try to help you even though we aren't crime lawyers, only maritime. Okay?"

I didn't really understand all that but I got the gist of it. I finished my Coke and thanked him politely.

On my way out, I thanked the lady behind the desk.

"I'm sorry I bothered you with no appointment," I said.

"That's all right," she said, "it was a nice break in the everyday rigamarole."

That was a word I didn't know but it sounded like a good thing. I was finding out there are a lot of really nice people, you just have to find them.

Going down in the elevator, I thought about Lawyer Appleton saying that if the killer gets caught, my father would not have to be a material witness in jail anymore. Of course, it was not a sure thing that the fat killer would get nabbed but when you've got nothing, any news comes your way feels like something.

Mr. Arthur Conan Doyle was high up on my favorite list of authors and Sherlock Holmes was always saying solving this and that was elementary but I doubt there's a St. Louis police detective who'll make the J & J thing elementary. So I guess I should try to help out. Not that I'm a solving genius just because I read all the cases that Sherlock Holmes solved in *The Adventures of Sherlock Holmes,* but to coin a phrase, two hound dogs on the trail are better than one.

So to begin with I went back to where all this started, not knowing who or what I was looking for, but I knew I had to start somewhere. I could go to J & J and ask about the Bulova case but then they would know who I was and I couldn't snoop around. There was a boy on the corner next to a mound of *Post-Dispatch*es waving a paper in the air and calling out, "Get your *Post-Dispatch*!" I made my way over to him and asked if he needed any help. He was a big kid, fourteen or fifteen maybe, and he told me to get lost. I started to tell him my story and he listened but I kept getting interrupted by people getting papers. Finally he said, "Why'd they cuff your pop?"

Said I didn't know. Asked if he knew who the man was got killed.

"Mr. Dempsey. Nice guy. Used to slip me an extra nickel now and then. My pop knew him."

"Who's your pop?"

"Worked at Scruggs. Got laid off. More'n a year ago."

"Lucky you got this job."

"Yeah."

"What about your mom?"

"Died from the influenza back when everyone had it. You got a mom?"

"Yeah, she's sick in a sanitarium."

"What's wrong?"

"Consumption. Second time."

"What's that?"

"Don't know exactly. Spots on her lungs and lots of coughing with blood. She can maybe die."

It was hard talking with him having to yell "*Post-Dispatch*! Get your *Post-Dispatch*!" and handling the coins. He told me his name, Augie Beckmier, said he'd try to get me a job like his if I wanted.

I said no, thanks, because I had to try to find the killer and I was hoping he would help me. He said to come back in an hour when the boy who spelled him usually showed up.

WE WENT down the block to a place called Pete's Parlor where he ordered a root beer we shared with two straws. I asked him if he knew the people that worked at J & J. He said yes, he delivered papers to them every day. "Justin and Joel Jankman, the owners, they got a little office in the back. A guy in a cubicle does watch repair and there are three seller people, Dempsey was the one who handled money and stuff."

I asked him if he could get me their addresses. He said he thought he could since one of the sellers, Grace Dorso, was always very nice to him. "She's too fat and too jolly but nothing not to like."

"And the Jankmans?"

"Justin's all right, makes jokes and kids with me. Joel's a real dump. All about himself. Grabs a paper, pats me on the head, never pays, says catch you next time. Big load of blue-ribbon bullshit."

"But with everybody all over hitting bottom how can the Jankmans—"

"Wedding rings. People scrape up their last dollar, starve, to get a wedding ring, especially one with diamonds. They probably go straight from their honeymoon to a pawnshop but the J brothers get the whipped cream off the top."

"You think everybody at J & J knew my father and his watches were coming in at three o'clock?"

"Probably. That's usually when salesmen come in."

"Did you see the murderer going in or out of the store?"

"Nope. My job doesn't leave me much time for gawking around. But I'll help you any way I can. We are a couple a guys with pop trouble."

"Does your pop do anything?"

"No. He's given up trying. He had a little spot on the sidewalk off Washington near Fifth selling apples for five cents but there were apple guys all up and down the street with signs like

'Help Feed My Hungry Kids' and sometimes he'd spend a whole day sitting behind his apple sign and still have all the apples he started with."

"Same as my father and his glass candlesticks. Couldn't give them away. Now he finally gets a job—"

"My pop's given up looking for work. He tried everything, everywhere, all he got was no, no, no, finally he just seemed to melt down. I mean from the pop I knew, I mean he was a great man, we went to ball games and played touch football and movie nights and all kinds of good stuff but then Mom died and . . ."

He took a long pull on his root-beer straw. His voice got all choked up. I thought he was finished but he pushed his voice back.

"Now he is all the time sad and to pay the rent and buy our food he has to sell my mom's jewelry, all the things he gave her the sixteen years they were married, one at a time and every time he has to take something out of her jewelry box, he cries, I mean, sits there in the kitchen with the bracelet or the ring and he can't stop his crying. I guess each thing reminds him of the time he gave it to her, where they were, all that stuff. He really loved my mom."

I said that my father had the same thing with

a brown diamond ring he gave my mom that she loved and he is trying hard not to sell it even though she wants him to. He once cried when Nathan the pawnbroker almost sold it.

The root beer was gone and I thought it was high time to change the subject.

"Augie, when you go into J & J to deliver the paper, can I go in with you? I'd like to see those people and maybe locate my father's watch case."

"Sure," he said. "Come on. We can do it right now."

We went back to his newsstand. Augie took several newspapers and gave me a couple. He waved to the boy who had taken over.

I followed Augie into the J & J. There were two people standing at a glass counter looking at several wedding rings spread before them on a black velvet cloth. Behind the counter was one of the three sellers Augie had mentioned, name of Grace Dorso. A kind of chubby lady with bright circles of rouge on her cheeks. There was a little cubicle with a man hunched over an opened watch, a small glass squished in his eye. The two other sellers stood behind an empty glass case so I guess it was the one that was robbed. The man was very dapper, striped suit with a little handkerchief peeking out of his dress pocket, a high, stiff collar, and a tie with red, white, and blue stripes. The other seller was a gorgeous young woman, like movie gorgeous with bright red fingernails and lipstick that matched. They said hi to Augie as he gave them their papers. He introduced me as his assistant. I gave one of my papers to the gorgeous movie star.

As I walked around I looked as best I could for a sign of the Bulova case but saw nothing.

We left and I asked Augie what he knew about these people. He knew that Joel was married, no kids, big fancy house and car. Justin married with kids, nothing fancy. The beauty, Bonnie Porter, marriage diamond on her finger, but Augie knew nothing about the watch-repair guy, Sol Greenblatt.

"And the guy in the swell clothes?"

"Oh that's Matt J. Pringle, been here forever, gives out cards with his face on 'em."

"Listen, Augie, one of these J & J people may have been in cahoots with the killer. Would you help me find out about them?"

"Like who?"

"Like the Pringle guy."

"What about him?"

"Follow him home without his knowing. Who he lives with. How he lives. Anything looks sig-

nificant. Any sign of guns around. Anybody vis-
ited could be the killer? All kinds of stuff like
that."

"I see him take the number twelve streetcar
every day at six."

"Get on it with him. But don't let him see
you."

"Sure. But how'll I get in touch with you?"

"You can't. I haven't got a place right now. But
I'll be in touch with you."

Which reminded me, I had to line up somewhere for the night, and it wouldn't be on top of
the tennis nets in the shed in Forest Park with
mice tickling my toes.

Happening 12

Connecting with Augie was a big plus for me, not only was he going to detectify on Mr. Pringle, but his life was pretty much like mine, only difference his mother was dead and his father wasn't in jail.

I thought I might stick around and detectify Sol Greenblatt when he left work but I decided it was more important to go back to the Tremont, check with Vernon on the Ford, and pick up letters from my mother who wrote me just about every day. She had a wonderful handwriting and just seeing it—the way she floated her *y*s and her *g*s—was a little like having her right there.

I checked our door to see if the notice was still there—it was—and I went across the courtyard down to Vernon's place in the basement. The door was open and I could smell his cooking. I went in calling out his name but he wasn't alone. A large woman all in black holding a stuffed briefcase was talking to him. Soon as he saw me he called out, "Hello, Stanley, your toilet stuffed up again?"

For about three seconds I thought Vernon had gone gaga but when the woman turned to look at me with her super-spooky face and a tag on her said "Freda Muller, Juvenile Welfare," I caught on and said, "My father wants to borrow your plunger."

"Sure thing," Vernon said, handing me a plunger.

"You know Aaron Broom in 12B?" the woman said to me in a cannon of a voice that would make drill sergeants wet their pants.

"No, ma'am," I said creakily. "I mean, yes, I know him but—"

Vernon cut in quick. "It's okay, George, I already told Missus Muller that Aaron's not—"

"I thought this was Stanley!" she blasted with her cannon again.

"Oh, yeah, get him mixed up with his twin brother," Vernon said.

"We're identical," I said. "I'm Stanley, all right."

She gave me a look that would kill a battalion of wild gorillas, turned back to Vernon. "Find him!" she commanded in a blast that could derail a train and left. Vernon reached inside an old teapot and took out a bottle of whiskey.

"That woman prob'ly caused the De-pression," he said and tilted the bottle into his mouth. "Damn woman drove me off the wagon." He exhaled and plunged the cork back in the bottle with a thump.

"Coupla letters from your mama," he said, handing them to me, "and this package from the Windy City Hosiery but your pa's not here to deliver it."

"I'll tell her," I said. "Meanwhile you hang on to it. How's Bertha?"

"All safe and sound. Sleepin' like a baby behind them tires. How 'bout a dish a my turnip stew? Looks like you ain't partakin' much."

I wasn't a big fan of turnips but my poor stomach had a welcome sign out for any contribution.

He served it up with a slice of Wonder Bread and my stomach gave it a standing ovation.

"Guess there's no way for me to get those quarters out of the Fatima tin, is there?"

"Nope. If I was you, I would try to keep my distance until they take down that sign from your front door. But I can lend you a little somethin' if you like."

"No, thanks, Vernon, but in these times a delicious plate of turnip stew is better than a two-dollar bill popping up on a huckleberry bush."

Happening 13

I sat on a bench in Forest Park and read my mother's letters, one by one, slowly, taking my time to feel her being with me. Despite her being in a dismal world of coughers and die-ers, she tried to sound cheerful or at least hopeful that she would soon be well enough to come home but I could tell that she was covering up the pain of being away from us and that she really didn't know when she would be able to leave the sanitarium. It's like when you play hardball and the pitcher plunks you in the rump with a fastball and knocks you down and you get up hurting like all hell but you mustn't rub the hit spot or make a hurt face and you jog to first base as if you were just fine even though you're not.

No two ways about it, I must go out to see her even though visitors are not allowed inside the sanitarium because consumption is very catchable, so I'll just holler up to her from the lawn outside.

THE WAY to get to the Fee-Fee Sanitarium, you take the Creve Coeur trolley to the end of the line. It was a really nice ride. Trees and country all the way through Creve Coeur and we even passed a lake where men with straw hats were fishing.

It was quite a walk from the trolley stop to the sanitarium and I passed many nice houses with clothes drying in their backyards. Made me aware that I looked pretty rumpled and scruffy, not a pretty sight for my mom who always had something washed clean for me to put on. But I didn't want her to know anything about our place being locked up or Pop in jail so I did what I had to do—I kept an eye on those backyards and found one that had kids' clothes hanging that looked just about my size. Making sure no one was watching or a dog about to tear me apart, I plucked a pair of socks, underwear, a shirt, and pants from the clothesline and took them where I changed behind a tree for cover, leaving all my things on the ground. I really wasn't stealing anything since my stuff would replace what I took once it was washed. Matter of fact my shirt was a lot nicer than the one I took. So I think it was okay for me to pick some of their flowers and I'd have a bouquet to give to my mother.

Happening 14

My mother was on the second floor of a white frame building that had a screen porch running all around it. There was bed after bed after bed all along this screen, and all you heard was coughing, the kind where something comes up at the end. My father had explained to me that the cure for my mother was lots of fresh air and sunshine and things like cream and eggs to eat.

I finally located her by walking around the building and looking up at people in the beds. She was very glad to see me, and me to see her. I held up my flowers and showed her I'd send them up to her. It wasn't very private talking to her with everybody in their beds from the first floor and second floor listening. They didn't have anything else to do, so they just looked out at me and listened. I felt like I was on the stage. There were lots of other visitors standing on the lawn talking up to people in the beds but I swear everyone was listening to me.

While we were talking I could see that some patients were walking along the aisles between the beds with tin cups in their hands. When they coughed and brought stuff up, they spit into the tin cups. The people in the beds had tin cups, too, that they spit into, but all the time I was there my mother never coughed once.

I told her that Father was on the road somewhere but that I was making out just fine. I made up a lot of stuff like that. She complimented me on how neat and clean I looked. I stayed on the lawn trying to think of things to talk about until the bell rang that meant visitors had to leave. I had almost forgotten to tell her that a shipment from the Windy City Hosiery Company had arrived. This bothered her.

"Oh, dear," she said, "I'd forgotten. They have to be delivered."

"I'll deliver them," I said.

"No, I don't think you should."

"Why not? It's in East St. Louis, isn't it? Well I know where East St. Louis is."

My mother was suddenly upset which wasn't good for her. I was sorry I told her about the Windy City package.

"Well, I guess I have to send you, A," she said.

"Okay."

"You just go there and then right home, hear? Oh, if only your father were here to do it." I couldn't imagine why she was so upset. It wasn't a big package and God knows it wasn't heavy with all those silk things in it, and if I could get myself to Creve Coeur I could certainly get myself to East St. Louis.

"Well I guess it will be all right, but be careful changing streetcars. When you collect the money, twenty dollars goes to the company. You just take it to the post office and get a money order. The two-seventy-five commission—you keep the seventy-five cents and mail me the two-dollar bill inside a folded paper so no one can see the money through the envelope."

We waved goodbyes and threw kisses. I went to the man at the door and he said he would send my flowers up to her.

I STARTED on my way back to the trolley, full of the sadness of seeing her like that. Having to pretend that we were just fine when we weren't. I felt heavy, like my legs couldn't carry me. I was passing a bench and I collapsed on it. The tears flooded out of me. I am not a crier. I never cry. I can keep hurt inside. But I was crying and drawing in to breathe and saying things to myself I had never said before. It was like the time I had a boil and the nurse at school lanced it and all the bad stuff inside came running out.

GOING BACK on the trolley was a very heavy ride. Leaving her alone with all those coughing people. What a wonderful woman she was, how in her quiet, firm, loving way she held us together and although we had nothing and nothing to look forward to, my mother convinced my father and me that we were going to survive the endless days without hope. Somehow she kept us from resenting the better life of some people, even making me feel in some ways superior to kids in school who were much better off. She could stitch up a worn-out patch in my pants in such a way made me feel that she was giving me a new pair of pants. I hope that's what all good mothers do. I can only speak about mine. Why she's being cruelly punished is something I can't understand. Right now it does not seem, as my mom says, that someone is watching over us, but if there is, considering my father's in jail, my mom's locked away with consumption, and me hunted by freaky Freda Muller, I wish he would please watch over someone else for a while.

I went to Vernon's place to pick up the Windy City Hosiery package, making sure Freda Muller wasn't lurking around. The way she kept after me, you would think I was Jack the Ripper.

I changed streetcars at the Eads Bridge, which crossed the Mississippi to the Illinois side where East St. Louis is located. As the streetcar headed toward the bridge we passed through a zillion shacks in a Hooverville that was packed into the approach area before the start of the bridge. There were all kinds of shelters—tents big and little; packing containers; shacks of tin, cardboard, wood; food stands; a church made of rocks and bricks; and so on, a little dilapidated city, a place, I decided, where I could set up for the night.

I HAD never been in East St. Louis and one look at it made me wonder why anyone lived there when they could live across the Mississippi in St. Louis proper. It was dirty and ugly and all the men I passed in the street looked like they were packing guns or had a disease. Of course, St. Louis is dirty and some mornings the black coal smoke shuts out the sun and burns your eyes so bad it makes you cry, but East St. Louis made you *feel* dirty, if you know what I mean. And it was even hotter than St. Louis.

This street Betty Haskins lived on was not paved and had holes and gullies in it. I couldn't believe this is where the rich ladies lived who could afford to buy the Windy City silk things. I pushed the button over her name and waited in the East St. Louis sun with flies buzzing at me off the screen. Suddenly there was a click and a lady's voice said, "Hello, who's there?"

"I'm here to see Betty Haskins," I said.

"Who are you?"

"I have some things for her from the Windy City Hosiery Company. My mother is sick and I'm here to deliver them."

"Oh, sure, honey, whyn't you say so? Come on up." She buzzed me in.

A long flight of narrow stairs went up to the second floor. A very peculiar smell was pouring down the stairs from above. By the time I got to the top, I remembered the smell. There was a Gypsy lady around on Enright who had this fortune-telling parlor in the basement and I had smelled it there. I used to give out circulars for her, ten cents from after school to six o'clock, and she always had a thick stump of incense smoking away. Nobody much went to see her and she finally disappeared. When people aren't eating regularly, I guess they don't believe much in fortune-tellers.

When I got to the top of the stairs, I could scarcely see where I was. There were these dim orange lights with fringe shades over them and lots of beaded curtains. I was in a sort of corridor with several closed doors, and down at one end was a lighted room. I could hear voices and music coming from that room. One of the doors opened and a woman came out.

"Why, aren't you cute!" she said to me. "Are you Ina's boy?"

"Yes, ma'am."

"Too bad she's sick. Just bring the package in here."

I carried the package into her room and she shut the door. There were more orange lights there but I could see better. The room was all full of silks and satins, and there was a big bed in the middle with a silk canopy over it and gold angels at the corners holding the silk.

"Well, now, let's see what you brought. Just open it up on this couch."

Betty Haskins was a movie star. She had red hair and super-white teeth and she was wearing a black silk kimono with red flowers on it. My opinion of East St. Louis suddenly improved, because if someone that gorgeous who was rich chose to live here, there must be something to say for it. I opened the box and she started to take out things and lay them on the bed. She picked up a silk sort of nightgown, I guess it was, with lacy junk in front, and held it up against her and looked at herself in the wall mirror. It was pretty embarrassing.

"I can wait out in the corridor," I said.

"Oh you don't have to do that, honey," she said.

She looked at the bill and took some money from the center of her bra. I counted it and it came to exactly the right amount. A bell tingled and she went over to the wall where there was an earpiece hanging on a hook. She put it against her ear and talked into a talk place in the wall. "Hello who's there? . . . Oh, hello, honey, come right on up." She thanked me for coming, hoped my mother would be better, and opened the door for me. She certainly had good manners.

I put the money in my pocket, first checking

around with my fingers to be sure there weren't any holes in it, and I said goodbye and left. As I got to the stairs there was a fat man mopping his head with a handkerchief just coming up. He took a look at me and his eyes popped open. Going down those stairs it suddenly dawned on me where I was. I had read a book about a young woman named Nana by Émile Zola that was on the forbidden list at school, and also some absolutely forbidden stories by Guy de Maupassant, especially one about a woman who lived in a room with her little son, and when men would come up to visit her, she would hide her little son in the closet. She would put him on a chair and tell him to sit there and not make a sound. But one night he fell asleep and fell off the chair, and the man visiting his mother opened the door and saw him and was furious and stormed away without giving his mother any money. The little boy felt terrible and cried, but his mother was nice and loving and tried to make him feel better. I thought it was an absolutely wonderful story, but until that moment it was something that happened in faraway France and not in East St. Louis, Illinois.

There was a post office across the street from the Eads Bridge stop. I got a money order and two stamped envelopes, one that I addressed to the Windy City Hosiery Company, the other to my mom with a two-dollar bill I wrapped inside my post office receipt. I paid for the envelope and the money order fee from my seventy-five cents and that left me with two quarters that I hid in the lining of my felty that I always wore. It was really the crown of an old fedora hat someone had pitched as worthless. But I had scissored off the brim all around and cut a couple of air holes on the sides next to the big buttons with Franklin D. Roosevelt's face on them, left over from the election. I also had one small button in the back with Herbert Hoover's face that I had put a black X across.

Herbert Hoover was my father's worst enemy: "He's a liar, a fraud, a two-faced fathead who promises anything and produces *nothing*! A chicken in every pot, hah! A car in every garage! Yeah, and a Hoover bank that gobbles up every cent you save!" During the election, Franklin Roosevelt said about Hoover, "There is nothing inside the man but jelly," and after that Pop called him Jelly Hoover and I made up a jingle: "Hoover's got a big fat belly, Inside the man is only jelly." President Roosevelt said Mr. Hoover with his millions and all his millionaire friends blew up the government and buried all of us in the Depression and I believed him.

STANDING THERE outside the post office, hearing Pop in my head, I really and truly missed him and thought about how it was for him in jail. I had no idea where the jail was but maybe I could find out and go visit him and tell him that everything was going to be all right, give him hope, like President Roosevelt says, but how could I find the jail and maybe if I did Freda Muller might get tipped off and nab me.

An Olive streetcar came to a stop and I got on. Maybe if I had a talk with Augie, my new pal, I could get my detectifying back on track.

He was there, all right, hawking the *Post-*

Dispatch and we waved to each other. I saw that
a sign had been posted on the J & J window:

$500 Reward
For Information Leading to the Arrest
of
the Killer of Ted Dempsey
Reliable Insurance Company

I managed to talk to Augie while he moved
around his stand, selling his papers. He said
he didn't have a chance to tail Matt J. Pringle
because when he left J & J a flashy Marmon convertible with a beauty at the wheel picked him
up and they drove off.

"How were they?" I asked. "Kissy-kissy or
hand-shakey or what?"

"How were they?" he repeated. "Well, he
handed her something, she looked at it and
laughed as they drove away."

"That's all?"

"She pulled off her hat and shook out her
hair."

"Blond?"

"Black as the ace of spades."

Augie's replacement came and we went to

Pete's for a two-straw root beer, only this time I plunked down the nickel which came out of my original forty-seven cents. I was keeping the two quarters in my felty liner an untouched secret.

"So what do you think of this Pringle guy?" Augie asked.

"Well from the way he dressed, all starchy and bankery-looking, I never had him pegged as a ladies' man, did you?"

"Yup, I did."

"How come?"

"When I took you into J & J he was showing a diamond bracelet to a woman and the way he was holding her hand to fit it on."

"Sexy?"

"Very. She was mooning at him. He gave her his card."

"Even so how has that anything to do with—"

"Look, Aaron, we're just a couple a kids. If I were a grown-up I'd a hopped in my car and tailed them and maybe got some clues but—"

"But you did get a clue, just in her picking him up. Listen to me, Augie, that fat guy who peeled off the wall and slid behind my father was somebody who knew Dad was coming at three o'clock and the only way he could have known that is if someone at J & J had tipped him off. We find who that was, we find the killer."

"Yeah, I know. But besides the J & Js there's one other person the cops are looking at."

"Who?"

"Your pop."

"What!"

"I know, I know, he's your pop but if you're detectifying you have to consider that he's down and out, owes a lot of money, wants to get his ring from the pawnshop, so there's this guy he knows that wants to rob the J & J so all your father has to do is tell him the time and the guy promises him a payoff. That's how these things work."

"My father wasn't into anything like that. No way!"

"I'm not saying he was, it was just a for-instance."

"Well I'm still going to detectify on the others. That Grace person, so jiggly and giggly and she's pretty darn nervous."

"How do you know?"

I almost said "Elementary, my dear Augie," but I held back and all I said was she nibbles her fingernails clear off. "I'd like to find out why she's so nervous. And I'd also like to know how come a beauty like Bonnie Porter, who's quite a lady, works here in a nothing job wearing all those beautiful clothes."

"One thing I can tell you, she's married to an actor who does radio stuff on KMOX and acts at the Muny. Their pictures are in the paper at special events."

"If you ask me she's covering something up."

"How do you know?"

"Inhibition."

"What?"

"Inhibition."

"You mean intuition?"

"Crap! Why do I get these mixed up?"

"Listen don't knock yourself. For a twelve-year-old you do all right."

"Thirteen is getting very close."

"We'll celebrate with root beer and hot dogs on me."

I noticed his straw had slurped up more than mine. "You know what? We stay at it we might just get lucky."

"Yeah, lucky, we sure haven't had a ton of that."

Happening 17

The Eads Bridge Hooverville looked different now that I was on the ground than it did when we passed over it in the trolley. What seemed to be a packed jumble of rickety shacks one on top of the other was really rather organized. Everybody had their own space and there was a kind of open path where you could walk along the shacks from one end of the Hooverville to the other. It was a huge area starting on the ground below the ramp of the bridge and ending at the water. Some of the shacks had wobbly chairs and kiddie swings in front of them, and there were many with mounds made of bricks or stones where they could light a fire and cook. Even though the Mississippi water was at the end of the Hooverville, it was a far haul to get it to the main part of the camp, so the ground was coated in dust as was everything else. Enough water was carried in pails to wash clothes that hung from lines everywhere. Groups of kids played as best they could, with grown-ups sort of keeping an eye on them.

I walked through the camp taking all this in. It was getting dark now and some cooking fires were lit and the kids were being called to dinner. Several sheds had kerosene lamps burning. As I reached the center of the camp I came on a large group of Hooverville people listening to a radio. Seeing the radio made me aware that I hadn't heard any music and that everything was pretty quiet except for the noises kids made when they were playing.

This radio was an Atwater Kent same as the one we had at the Westgate until the tubes burned out and we didn't have the money to replace them. That's probably why nobody had their radio going—either busted tubes or the pawnshop or the fact that there was no electricity in the camp. This Atwater Kent was attached to a very long extension cord that was plugged into a light socket on the bridge high above. What was coming from the radio was President Franklin D. Roosevelt giving one of his fireside chats. It was turned up very loud and you could hear his voice all over, the way he talked, so easy-going and kind of confidential like he was talk-

ing directly to you, not speechifying like most
everyone else who's government. The people he
was talking to, all around me, had lost everything, their houses, their jobs, their cars, I mean
everything, just like we did, and yet here they all
were, having to live under the ramp of a bridge
in dirty shacks, their bellies as empty as mine,
huddled together, feeling good from listening
to FDR, just like me, more of us no better off
than we were when he got elected but when he
says it's all getting better we believe him, and
no one in this group leaves or boos when he says
things are a little better today than they were two
months ago. We applaud. He says two months
ago the country was dying by inches but we're
fighting back. Applause. Mortgages are being
saved. Applause. Young men with families being
put to work by the Civilian Conservation Corps.
Applause and whistles. Banks that were closed,
reopening. Applause. Farms saved. Applause.
And now thanks to a bill he has just signed we
can all drink beer! Biggest applause. (Two guys
drinking from bottles of Budweiser pass them
around.) That he and Congress, Democrats and
Republicans together, are now working hard to
stop all those things that came close to destroy-

ing our whole way of life. Applause and cheers. He says it's a good beginning but he needs us to believe together as we go forward.

Everyone cheered him and shared their good feelings as they started to go back to their shacks. Me too. I feel up not down even though I'm really hungry, I don't know where I'm going to sleep tonight, if I can detectify my father out of jail, and whether my mom might die in that sanitarium. But these were none of the things President Roosevelt could do anything about.

Happening 18

As I left the radio group, I became aware of, or I should say my stomach got stirred up by, a nifty aroma that was coming from a fire that was sending sparks floating up into the sky. As I got close to the fire I could see that it was coming from an oil drum that was burning hunks of wood. There were three boys standing around the drum, fourteen or fifteen, I guess, maybe couple a years more, eating pieces of potatoes that were roasting in the fire. If you ask me nothing beats the keen smell of a roasted potato with its crispy crunchy skin and its white crumbling inside especially if a little salt and butter can be forked its way.

"Whatcha lookin' at, kid?" one of the boys said. "You never seen a hot potato?" He was the biggest of the three, a lot taller than me.

"You've got a nice fire for the potatoes," I said. He tore off a hunk of the potato he was eating, holding it on a piece of newspaper. "Here, try a piece." I took the newspaper with the potato, thanking him. It burned my tongue a little but it was one hundred percent wonderful.

"My name is Jim," he said. "What's yours?"

"Aaron."

"Where's your brother?"

"I don't have—"

"Moses. Old Mo around?"

More potato would have been wonderful but I could tell big Jim was trouble and I started to leave. He grabbed me by the arm.

"Where you headed, Aaron? You haven't paid for that potato you ate."

"Okay, Jim, enough," one of the other boys said.

Jim kept a tight grip on my arm. "Tell you what . . ." He snatched my felty from my head and put it on his. "Perfect fit. Now we're even."

"Come on, Jim, why don't you pick on some-one your own size?"

"Yeah? Well why don't you put little Aaron on your shoulders? That should make him just about my size." He gave me a sharp bop on the top of my head with his fist that rattled my teeth.

I was feeling this rise in me I get when I have to defend myself. I forget the name of it but it like charges you up. He not only had my felty but he also had the quarters inside it.

"Whadaya say, Aaron, gonna get on Frank's shoulders and duke it out?" He gave me a sharp push and took a poke at my head. I saw his hand coming and I dodged it with a Vernon twist of my head. The other boys were yelling at him to cut it out but he poked at me with his other hand and I made him miss again. I was really fired up now, I mean all-out fired up, and before he could make another move on me I kicked him hard between his legs and he let out a yell and doubled over with short breaths and little cries and I took my felty off his head.

"Now I brought you down to my size," I said as I put my felty back on my head and walked away. The boy called Frank caught up with me. I feared it was maybe more trouble but he handed me a whole roasted potato rolled up in a double piece of newspaper.

"Thanks, Aaron," he said. "You did what we've been aching to do."

I FOUND a place to sit and ate the hot potato as slowly as my hunger would allow, trying to make it last as long as possible. I was sorry I had to use such a crude way to fight my way out of the bad spot I was in, but the years of the Depression had taught me you have to do what you have to do to survive, even if it's to kick a bully in the balls.

When I finished the potato, the empty newspaper in my lap and the sizzling St. Louis nighttime heat weighing me down, I felt empty. Not that the roasted potato didn't help, it did, but I could really eat a couple more. I mean empty like there's nothing ticking in me, the stuff that was making me believe that a twelve-year-old boy could detectify that killing and get his father out of jail and the lock off the door and the Ford out of hiding and the Bulova case returned. I was awful close to the one thing that I must not, must not, *must not* ever feel and that's sorry for myself. I'm not! I'm not any run-of-the-mill kid. I've been through a lot and I've learned a lot and I know who I am and what I can do and what I sure as sure can do is not feel sorry for myself! So I don't have a place to sleep tonight, zillions of people don't have a place or money or relatives or . . .

"Aaron!" I heard. "That you, Aaron?" Now I was hearing imaginary voices.

The imaginary voice belonged to a girl who

came up to me and gave me a big hug. I couldn't believe my eyes.

"Ella, oh, Ella!" I said as she laughed and we both said at the same time, "Are you living here?"

Ella McShane and her mom had lived two rooms away from ours at the Westgate Hotel. Ella was three years older and a head taller. We were good friends and she told me about all the places they had lived when her father was with them and he was sent to those places for his work. Ella was very smart and she read a lot but she had epilepsy and couldn't go to school. Her father no longer lived with them but he sent money so they could buy special medicine for her epilepsy with a little money left over so they could get some food and maybe pay some rent. They had left the Westgate before we did but I can't remember if they were locked out like we were or just decided to leave.

Ella and I walked to her place so I could see her mother, a swell woman who sometimes helped my mom when she was sick. They lived in one of the better Hooverville shacks, a large, solid square tent that had cots and a little kitchen and place for a table and two chairs. They even had a few pictures on the wall. There was a kerosene lamp on the table and a spot where they kept bathroom things. They also had a Victrola you could crank up by hand. Ella had a nice voice and she knew a lot of songs. At the Westgate she had wanted me to sing along with her but at school I was even banned from singing "America the Beautiful" because I was told I had a voice that made all the other voices sound bad.

Mrs. McShane was every bit as nice as I remembered her. She served us raisin cookies and asked all about me and my family.

"But, Aaron, aren't you a little young to get grown-ups to take you seriously?"

"That's the whole point," I said. "The murderer might talk to a kid like me."

"Well, just be careful, kill once, kill twice, you know. Maybe you should keep track of things." She took a little notebook from a drawer in the table and handed it to me along with a stub of a pencil. I thanked her and put them in my back pocket. "You be careful, hear?"

"Oh, yes, ma'am, I always make sure who's behind me."

"Now, let's get to the immediate. You've got to have a place to sleep. As you can see, we are squished in here as is."

"Oh, don't you worry about me, Mrs. McShane," I said. "I have a place in Forest Park if I want."

Ella had a package of cinnamon gum and was offering me a stick when it happened. The first thing I knew, her arm went stiff-out and she let out a little scream and fell to the floor. She was making a kind of grunting noise, and I was petrified. Her whole body was very stiff and I could see the rolled-up whites of her eyes, and her legs were jerking like someone was poking something hot at her feet. I was really scared to death.

Her mother ran to the table and got something and ran back to Ella. It was a stick like the nurse at school used to look down your throat. Mrs. McShane poked the stick into Ella's mouth. "Quick, Aaron, quick!" she said to me. "Raise her head, she's swallowing her tongue!" I bent down and picked up Ella's head and Ella's mother kept working the stick in her mouth till she pulled her tongue out. Ella's body was jerking all over now, and she was making little crying noises and she broke wind several times. I wanted to help. Oh God how I wanted to help, but I didn't know what to do.

Then just as suddenly as it had started, it

ended. All at once. Her eyes came back in place and she relaxed and her body smoothed out. Her mother took a wet cloth and wiped her face, and then we helped her to her feet. I picked up her glasses and handed them to her.

"Are you all right, dear?" her mother asked.

"Oh, sure," she said, trying to smile. She was very white and she had freckles I hadn't noticed before.

"I'd better be getting on," I said, and I thanked Mrs. McShane for the cookie. I felt terrible. Really terrible.

"I'm sorry," Mrs. McShane said to me. "Ella hasn't had one of those for a long time."

"Was it awful?" Ella asked me. She was holding her fingers together very tight.

I didn't know what to say.

"Now, Ella, let Aaron be on his way."

"I just want to know if I did anything really bad," Ella said, her voice louder.

"Well," I said, wanting to die, "you were sick and now you're all right."

"Here," she said, "you didn't take your gum." She offered me the stick of cinnamon gum which she still had in her hand. I took it and put it in my pocket.

"I didn't have my medicine," she said. "I'm all right as long as I take my medicine."

"I was a dollar short," Mrs. McShane said, "and the druggist refused, even though I promised to pay as soon as my money came. Even offered to leave my watch."

"Do you have the empty package your last medicine came in?" I asked. "And a prescription?"

"Yes," Ella said. "I have the empty bottle in it."

"Is the pharmacy near here?" I asked.

"Yes. Two blocks down."

I said, "I've got an idea."

THE EADS PHARMACY was busy. A few of the Hooverville people were there. I gave the prescription to the woman at the pharmacy desk. She disappeared and came back with the package of medicine. She put it on the counter in front of us and told me to take it to the cashier. The cashier totaled up the charge. I looked at the bill and said, "There must be a mistake. We never pay that much, do we?" I said to Ella.

"I should say not," she said.

"That's the charge," the cashier said. "Take it or leave it."

"But my sister absolutely needs the medicine," I said, laying it on thick. "Life or death."

"Sorry, but that's it. Take it or leave it."

"All right," I said, "I guess we have to leave it."

The cashier put the package on the shelf behind her. "Next," she said.

We went back to Ella's shack and opened the package with the new bottle of pills that I had exchanged for the empty one I had taken from my pocket. Ella swallowed a pill and it seemed to improve her spirit.

"You're a lifesaver, Aaron," Mrs. McShane said.

"The way he did it, Mom, smooth as Jell-O. And to think of switching like that."

"I can't take credit," I said. "I watched my father get my mother her medicine that way."

"I had an idea while you were gone," Mrs. McShane said. "Have you seen Captain Arnold lately?" she asked Ella.

"No, not for some time."

"Anyone been there?"

"No, don't think so."

"Well," Mrs. McShane said to me, "you may be in luck. Captain Arnold's an old navy grouch who has that patch back there where the hammock is. He spends his day at the navy retreat on Market but he's slept in that hammock in his space every night for as long as we've been here. Shows up same time every evening. Never says a word to us or anyone else. Has no friends or family so maybe he's navigated his way to navy heaven. Why don't you take over? Worst thing could happen is he shows up and kicks you out. But he's always been here hours before now."

I had never been in a hammock and the way it weaved when I tried to get into it, my first attempts landed me on the ground. I finally settled in but I had a little trouble falling asleep because I was afraid I would spin over in the night and break my neck. But, fact is, I never had a better sleep and fortunately the captain did not show up and deliver a klop or two because my head was still a little sore from the bops rained down on me from big Jim.

That morning I left quickly so that the McShanes didn't have to feel they had to offer me some breakfast, if they had any. Just outside the Hooverville I found a small variety shop where I got two pancakes and a glass of milk plus a toothbrush and a little sample tube of Pepsodent, all for seven cents.

Happening 19

As I got off the Olive Street trolley I saw Augie waving at me.

"She's in J & J," he said. "Take a look."

I went over to the J & J window with its $500 reward sign, and there was Pringle bent over a glass counter full of diamond things, with a beautiful flapper in a beaded dress also bent over the counter, a velvet tray between them. The flapper was trying on rings Pringle was handing to her that were lined up on the tray. She found one ring she liked, holding it up this way and that and then they came out of the door for her to see the ring in the outside light. They stopped a few feet from where I was standing. She smelled something wonderful.

While she was holding up her hand and admiring the ring in the hot St. Louis sunshine, she reached in her sparkly bag that was hanging on her shoulder and took out something that she handed to him. I couldn't make out what it was.

They both started to laugh and returned to the store. Pringle tidied up all the rings and put them back into the glass case, all except the one on the flapper's finger. She took it off and he shined it up with a special cloth, then she put it back on. He walked her to the door, they shook hands goodbye, and she got into her Marmon convertible that was double parked at the curb. A man wearing a linen cap and driver's gloves with cut-off fingers was at the wheel and he drove away as soon as she closed the door.

AUGIE AND I went down to Pete's to share a cheese sandwich and a root beer (no longer called Pete's Parlor but changed to Pete's Pub when beer became legal).

"What was that all about?" I said. "No money, no papers . . ."

"She gave him something."

"He didn't even look at it. Did he put it in his pocket? Or his drawer?"

"Dunno. Just disappeared."

"So who is this Pringle?"

"Dunno. But that's probably not his real name."

"I think you're right. He sounds fishy, all flashed up like that."

"I'll try to tail him again tonight."

"She probably won't be picking him up."

Two men came into Pete's and sat down at the bar. They wore straw boaters and seersucker suits. Augie nodded his head in their direction.

"What?"

"Justin and Joel," he whispered.

They didn't look like brothers. The bartender drew two foamy beers and put them in front of the brothers along with a bowl of peanuts. I once had a sip of beer, thought it tasted like awful medicine you don't want to take. Our little table was near the bar, J & J's backs to us, and we could hear everything they were saying.

"What do you think about the insurance guy?"

"He pretty much okayed everything on our list, didn't he?"

"Yeah, but the head office can always chop it down some."

"Hope not but we do have something to worry about."

"What's that?"

"Whoever beat our guy to the snatch. When that bastard discovers that stuff he stole was all fakes, what's he going to do? If our guy had made the grab as we planned, we'd a got rid of it but now it's a ticking bomb. He could make a deal with the insurance company. They pay him for our fake stuff and then nail us for fraud, maybe put us out of business and into the clink."

"You may be right. So, listen, we can't take their money, anyway, not now, put it off, but we got to catch the guy who shot Dempsey and grabbed our stuff. One of our employees must have tipped him off that three o'clock—"

"Could also be that Bulova watch guy—"

"The cops say they're working him over."

Hearing that hit me a jolt. "Working him over!" I repeated. Augie clapped his hand over my mouth.

"Shhhh!" he whispered.

A lot of people were coming into Pete's now and the place was filling up.

"But Joel," his brother was saying, "we gotta have the insurance money."

"I know."

"We promised him."

"I know."

"God knows what he'll do."

"We just got to stall and take our chances."

"You handle it. I'm no good trying to deal with him."

"Maybe we could just sell all the good stuff for a lump sum, pay him off, and be done."

"And then how do we stay in business and out of the clink palming off paste for diamonds?"

The phone at the bar rang. "It's for you, Mr. Joel," the barman said, handing him the phone. Joel listened, then put down the phone.

"We've got to get back," he said to his brother. They hurriedly paid up and left.

I asked Augie what he thought that meant, "working him over."

"All that stuff they do—bright lights, a million questions, no sleep—you've seen the movies."

"Sometimes they knock 'em around, don't they?"

"Look, Aaron, you can go nuts worrying over what might be or not be. If you want to really help your dad let's put our heads on what we just heard."

He was right, of course, but my head was not in very good shape. "You're right," I said, pushing myself. "Seemed to me the brothers need cash to pay some tough somebody, so they took the good stuff out of that case and put in fakes and hired a guy to rob the case, making off with all the fakes, but they collect insurance money as if what he took was the real thing."

"Right. But someone got there first and grabbed the fakes not knowing they weren't stealing the real stuff. Whoever that was, he knew your pop was coming at three o'clock and that the door would be buzzed open for him."

"So now this guy shoots Dempsey who's trying to shoot him while he's grabbing things and off he goes with a bag full of fake jewelry, thinking he's hit the jackpot."

"So the brothers are now worried that he might go to the insurance company and spill the beans about the fakes if they don't tell the cops about him so he wouldn't get nailed for shooting Dempsey. Looks like you're getting into some pretty scary stuff."

Yeah, he was right, some pretty scary stuff, but so is my father into some pretty scary stuff and I'm the only one on the outside who can maybe help him with my detectifying.

There was a kind of code of honor, I guess you'd call it, in the Hooverville, not to hang around anyone's place when they were cooking. Maneuvering for a handout or looking for a sympathetic this or that was strictly not allowed. I was told there was a group of Hooverville enforcers who could kick you out even if you had an okayed shack. So I made certain to show up at my hammock after Ella and her mom had cooked, even though Mrs. McShane had told me to come by any time because they could always rustle up a little extra.

So I'd already had a plate of spaghetti at Gino's in Dago Hill, five cents with tomato sauce, six cents with crumbly cheese. I'm very partial to spaghetti, it fills all the crannies of my stomach. When I went to my hammock I had already brushed my teeth and washed my face at the Hooverville basin. I took off my Keds and settled in. I hadn't seen Ella but hand-wound music was coming from their tent-shack and they had their kerosene lamp lit. The night was extra St. Louis hot and the hammock strings were frying my back. Luckily the mosquitoes were passing me up.

I lay there looking through the heat at the stars, thinking about what the J & J brothers said at Pete's and how little I could really do about any of it. I thought about Captain Arnold and how maybe he was dead and had put this hammock in his will and that someone might show up to claim it. I tried hard not to think about my father or my mother both of them suffering but that pushed me down in the dumps and erased my sleepiness so I decided to steer off downers and try to remember some good things I could sleep on like the championship game our school won that I pitched and held them without a score by throwing very close inside pitches that made them scared of being hit, and hitting a few of them on the shoulders and butts to keep the batters afraid of me. Our school had never won a championship but the last inning, bases loaded, two outs, us leading only by one run, I struck out their best batter with a terrific inshoot that he swung at mightily and missed and my whole team came whooping to the mound and picked me up and put me on their shoulders and paraded me around all their parents and others coming down from the stands and cheering. A swell lift for a kid living in a one-room sad-ass hotel.

Made me think of another lift like that from my English teacher, Hilda Levy, now seeing her gentle face and fluffy white hair and hearing her polite voice talking about books and writers and the virtue of good spelling and the power of words. She liked the way I wrote my compositions. I loved her compliments. She encouraged me to play the dictionary game: open the dictionary every day to any page, find a word I didn't know, and get to know it. She was wonderful how she brought us into Shakespeare and into Latin. She also cared about me, myself. A couple of days before school let out for the summer, Mr. Stellwagon, the principal, came to our class and told us the sad news that she had died suddenly, making a dark Depression day darker.

Thinking about Hilda Levy being gone turned a good memory into a downer so I began to poke around in my head to find some lifter I could sleep on. I thought about the time I took up the violin using the school's violin since I didn't have one of my own, which meant I could only practice at school. But I found it easy to finger the notes of the violin and I got put in the Kennard School Orchestra. On parents' night when we played, the history teacher, Mr. Mathis, who was the conductor, gave me a solo section, a big honor, but when I stood up and put the violin under my chin and pulled the bow across the strings, two of them popped up from the bridge and hit me in the face so all I could do was sit down without playing a note. Not long after that music appreciation was dropped because of the Depression. Playing the violin was an upper but being bopped by the strings was humiliating and definitely a downer. I also relived that time with the Mexican dentist who had a little spot in the lobby of the hotel. I had a bad toothache and my father took me to him. It was a scruffy place that looked like it needed a lot of spit and polish. The dentist poked around and said my right lower molar was infected and needed to be drilled and filled or pulled.

"How much?" my father asked.

"Fifty cents fill, twenty-five pulled."

"Pulled," my father said, just like that, saving twenty-five cents.

"It won't grow again," the dentist said.

"He can chew on the other side."

So now I have a bare spot on molar row that the tip of my tongue doesn't like.

For crying out loud, I said to myself, dump the darn downers! Why do all my downers stick and the uppers don't? It's like on the radio and in the newspapers there's only bad things, murders, typhoons, and crooked senators but not much feel good, is there? Because we like to hear about misery and bad luck and things happening that aren't supposed to happen, like if Babe Ruth hits a home run that's ho-hum but if it's the ninth inning, two outs, and he strikes out with the bases loaded—headlines!

Well, that's when, for some reason, a wonderful upper came flooding back to me and carried me into my dreams. A couple a years ago, my mom still working at the Bell Telephone before I got her fired, we three went to a special New Year's Eve show at the Kingshighway Cinema that went from seven to midnight with everybody singing "Auld Lang Syne." The Kingshighway was once a vaudeville theater with a stage and orchestra pit so it was able to do special shows like this one that had a double feature, News of the World, short subjects, Mickey Mouse cartoons, a live orchestra with dancers and singers, and Follow

the Bouncing Ball with the whole audience singing. The Kingshighway cost twenty cents more
than the Tivoli, and in the summer it was "air-
cooled" which was big blocks of ice at the back of
the theater with large fans behind them blow-
ing toward the audience. I don't think it really
did much but it was better than the Tivoli which
moved into the parking lot outside the theater
and turned fans on the audience.

This New Year's Eve, my mom had made
meat-loaf sandwiches with potato salad and
pickles and pretzels and we bought a Coke in
the lobby that we shared. The movies were Fred
Astaire and Ginger Rogers in *The Gay Divorcee*,
and Marie Dressler and Wallace Beery in *Tug-
boat Annie*, both my favorites. The band played
toppers from the Hit Parade and a girl named
Tapioca Tilly did a lot of twirly tapping all over
the stage. Follow the Bouncing Ball featured
"On the Sunny Side of the Street" and I was surprised that my father had a terrific voice. He was
a serious, worried man and singing wasn't in his
nature. But the evening had lifted him from his
gloom and his "Sunny Side of the Street" carried
over the top of all the other voices in the theater.

It was the last time we shared an event as a
family.

Sol Greenblatt left J & J when it closed at six o'clock and took the number two streetcar headed toward the river, me right behind him but not too close for him to see me. It was a real surprise to see how tall and skinny and roomy in his clothes he was, sort of how I pictured Ichabod Crane when we read the Washington Irving story in school. Tell you the truth, I really liked the name Ichabod so much I nagged my father to let me change mine but when he found out he had to fill out forms and pay a fee at city hall that was the end of that. When Sol Greenblatt was all scrounged up at his little workplace, hunched over a watch with his magnifier screwed in his eye, it made him look like a small man, not at all like the guy that was now getting off at the Bellevue stop. Me too.

I had never been down here, bordering on the Mississippi. It was full of saloons and run-down houses that looked like no one lived in them but someone did. Some of the saloons had music and dancing and you could smell Mississippi fish frying. There were streetlamps but most of them were kaput and as it got dark it was hard to see where you were going. The river was full of passing barges and passenger steamers.

Sol Greenblatt knew his way around, winding from one place to another, and I tried to remember how he was going so's I'd be able to find my way back. He finally stopped at a saloon called Marcy's but did not go in. Instead he took a key from his pocket and unlatched a locked door beside the entrance. A few seconds later a light came on in the window of a room above the saloon. Sol took off his hat and suit coat and replaced them with a plaid cap and black vest. He took an envelope from his suit coat and put it in an inner pocket of his vest. Then he turned out the light and a few seconds later he came out onto the sidewalk. I hid behind a tree so's he wouldn't see me.

He turned to his right and walked along a row of night places, me following and stopping when he entered a dim spot called Finally. There were no streetlights. It was a black night with no moon or stars or anything. I found a small three-legged bench in the dark and set myself up with a view into Finally. Sol shared hugs with a pretty woman who was tending the bar that looked like it served a lot more than beer. She made a drink for him as a bright light came on above one of the tables. Several of the men who'd been sitting at the bar took their drinks and went to the table. So did Sol. The pretty bar woman came to the table with poker chips that she handed in equal piles to each man.

They began to play, dealing the cards and betting their chips. I didn't know enough about cards to know exactly what they were playing. Sol was very quiet, not looking at his down cards like the other men, but he seemed to be raking in most of the chips that were piling up in front of him. One time as he was pulling in some winning chips, it happened so fast I almost didn't see it, he reached inside his vest and passed his envelope to the man to his right, who pocketed it without looking at it. They stopped playing long enough for the men to fix up their drinks, and that's when Sol was suddenly beside me. I jumped.

"How you doing?" he said.

I wasn't able to say anything. I hadn't seen him leave the tavern or come to the bench.

"What's your name?"

I began to recover, but my heart was banging away.

"What's your name?" he repeated.

"Ichabod," I managed to say. He had a slight accent but I couldn't tell what.

"You're the kid came in with the newspaper boy."

"Yes, sir."

"Followed me tonight on the streetcar."

"Yes, sir."

"And to Marcy's."

"Yes, sir."

"Why?"

While I was yes-siring him I knew this why was on its way.

"Because I'm writing about the J & J shooting as my summer English project."

"You think you're going to solve it?"

"Oh, no, well, I'm just a twelve-year-old boy."

"And this is okay with your parents that you're down here?"

"They've gone away on an emergency."

"You're all alone?"

"No, I'm staying with friends."

"What friends?"

"The Hammocks."

"They picking you up?"

"No, I have a streetcar pass."

"Well, here I am—interview me."

"You're a swell cardplayer. Making all that money, why you have to work?"

"We don't play for money, we're all broke, we just play for the chips and the one who winds up with the most, the others have to pay his dinner. We all had jewelry stores and were fierce competitors but the big D put us out of business and now we are like a sad-ass fraternity."

"How come the J & J brothers can stay in business and you can't?"

"You better ask them. I warn you, they don't like to answer questions."

"They weren't there when the shooting happened?"

"Nope, neither one. That's something you can put in your story—first time I know of that one of them wasn't in the store. You also might want to talk to Grace who's so jolly and giggly all the time, and the beauty Bonnie Porter, who's always in the paper at the races with Roy Delray, the actor who's on KMOX and at the Muny. They are married. I can tell you, there is something fishy about J & J and you may get an A plus from your teacher if you write about all of that."

I asked him to tell me just what happened at

J & J on the day of the shooting. I took my pad and pencil out of my pocket to take notes and make me look like an eager beaver chomping for that A plus.

He said, "Well, the Bulova man showed up at the door at three o'clock and Dempsey buzzed him in. There had been so many robberies of jewelry stores since the Depression, the stores are now required to have buzzers to unlock the door for people to enter, and owners must let employees know when appointments are made. So in comes Bulova with his sample case followed right behind by a fat man with a heavy beard in overalls and a floppy tennis hat. Right away he pulls a revolver from his overalls pocket and says, 'Everybody freeze. Put your hands where I can see 'em, not up, just out in front.' "

"What does the Bulova man do?"

"Nothing. The fat man goes right to the number one case, knocks the lock off with the handle of his gun, takes a cloth bag from his pocket, and tells the Bulova guy to hold it open while he scoops up the stuff in the case and fills the bag."

"Exactly what does he say to Bulova? Call him by name?"

"Nope. Just 'hold this open.' Fat man shuts the top of the bag, he's wearing gloves, stuffs the sack

in his overalls and turns to go when Dempsey
shoots, misses, the front glass breaks, fat man
swings around, shoots, I duck down under the
counter, don't see anything more until the cops
arrive. Did you get all that?"

"I sure did. Did you see any more of the
Bulova man?"

"Nope. Cops took him away." Mr. Greenblatt
stood up and looked down at me. "Looks like you
could use something to eat."

"Oh, sir, I'm fine. Really."

"Come on."

He brought me to the bar and introduced me
to the pretty barmaid.

"Rosemary, this is Ichabod. He needs a juicy
hamburger and fries, on me." He left me with
Rosemary and went back to the card game.

Rosemary had shiny blue eyes and dimples
that showed up when she smiled at me. She was
putting a large hamburger on the grill.

"How you like it, Ichabod? Medium?"

"Yes, please."

"Ketchup?"

"Yes, please."

"Pickles?"

"Yes, please."

"Onions?"

"Yes, please."

"Relish?"

"Yes, please."

"Mustard?"

"Yes, please."

"French fries?"

"Yes, please."

"Cheese?"

"Yes, please."

"Tomato?"

"Yes, please."

She served it at the bar, the most wonderful sight my eyes had ever seen. Rosemary made herself a drink and talked to me as I wolfed down the loaded burger and the fantastic fries. While I was eating, the card game ended. Sol came to the bar and sat down beside me.

"So you're going to interview everyone who works in the store?"

"Yes, sir."

"You want their home addresses?"

"Oh, yes, sir."

"You better be careful. You may be getting yourself into a little trouble."

"I hope not."

He wrote down their addresses.

"You think one of them might have tipped off the three o'clock shooter?"

"Sure."

"Which one?"

"Any one of them. Think you can find your way back to the streetcar?"

"Oh, sure."

He shook my hand and I thanked him for the burger and the interview. Rosemary gave me a big hug and a kiss on both cheeks even though I was reeking of onions.

When I got back to the Hooverville I found a note from Ella pinned to my hammock asking me to dinner the next night. It said her mom was making chili con carne, one of my favorites.

Using water from a bottle I kept hidden under old newspapers, I brushed my teeth, kicked off my Keds, and swung myself into the hammock, feeling kind of depressed. As a detectifier I had been a flop. I didn't fool Sol Greenblatt one bit. He knew I was tailing him, and for all my dumb questions, I didn't find out anything that would help me. I didn't even discover anything about Sol himself, anything might make me think he could be the three o'clock tipster I was looking for. Instead all I got was his card game and Rosemary and that luscious hamburger.

So now I'll have to get to the other three people in the store and detectify something that would lead me to the killer—about as easy as swimming from here to New Orleans under water. But as I began to get drowsy I remembered something Hilda Levy once told me about the great books we were reading. I could hear her voice in my head as clear as rain: "Aaron, when things get looking bleak, you can always cheer up by expecting the unexpected."

THE NEXT DAY I felt the best thing I could do while waiting for the maybe unexpected was to hang around J & J and watch the comings and goings. Augie gave me some papers to tuck under my arm so's I'd blend in with the crowds. Of course any papers I actually sold I'd turn the money over to him. I could see the usual J & J people Grace, Matt, and Bonnie doing their jobs, selling things to customers, Sol Greenblatt hunched over his watch table. I don't think he noticed me but if he did he didn't show it.

Augie had gone into Scruggs to use the men's room and I was alone on the corner when KAZOOM! the unexpected reared up. I was on the sidewalk at the curb, shouting up the *Post-Dispatch*, when a really classy REO with dark windows came zooming to a stop right where I was, a back door flew open, someone got pushed into the gutter, and the REO took off as soon as the door slammed shut.

The guy in the gutter who I thought might be dead pushed his arm up at me and said, "Hey, kid, gimme a hand." I put down my papers and grabbed hold of his hand and tugged him. He had some blood on his face, around his nose, and his suit was a little torn but with me helping he was able to stand up. That's when I saw it was one of the J & Js, Justin, the smaller, skinnier one. There were drops of blood on his necktie. He was holding hard on to my arm.

"I gotta get to Pete's," he said.

I saw Augie coming back from Scruggs and gave him the high sign. There were people moving back and forth on the busy sidewalk but no one was paying any attention to us, like a guy who could barely stand up, with blood on him and his clothes torn was everyday stuff.

No questions asked, Augie took Justin's other arm and he leaned on us as we helped him down the street into Pete's. We walked him past the bar and the front tables into the dining area where there were about a dozen tables with checkered tablecloths, most of them busy. There was a swing door that led to the kitchen and another door that was locked with a man sitting outside it. Justin steered us toward him and as soon as the man saw Justin he opened the locked door and took his arm and led him inside, the door closing behind them.

On our way back to the newspapers, I told Augie about the black REO and the way Justin had been dumped in the gutter.

"What's behind that door?" I asked Augie.

"Pete's speakeasy. That's where all the big bootleggers hang out. And rich guys with keys and flashy girls."

"What about Justin?"

"There's all kind of people. Supposed to be the best booze around."

"And the cops don't care?"

Augie laughed. "You don't know much do you? Anyway, speakeasies are going under now with repeal."

Augie was right. I didn't know much. Like speakeasy, I heard of it but really didn't know what it was. Same for bootleggers. What kind of detectifier doesn't know about those things?

We were back at Augie's corner and he scooped up the coins that had been left on top the papers. Even in hard times like these, people left their nickels when they didn't have to.

I went back to where I was when Justin landed in the gutter. I had a feeling that sort of drew me back there. A feeling that sometimes comes over me and makes me go places and do things. I think it's hooked up with moving around so much. I read about nomads and Gypsies and I think I must have some of that in me. How else can you explain why I took myself back to that spot in the gutter where Justin had landed, where I helped him up. There in the gutter half covered with chewed-up cigar butts and candy wrappers was a billfold, a fresh billfold. I didn't make a dive for it. Too many eyes around. There was a guy sitting behind a five-cent apple sign on the sidewalk right across the street. What I did was sit down on the curb and slowly, without looking, fish around the guck in the gutter, get my fingers on the wallet, and slide it into my pocket. A car honked at me—someone wanted to park in my spot.

WHEN I told Augie I had to see him in absolute privacy, he said to follow him to a little closet in the back of a candy-and-cigarette store on the corner, where he stored his newspapers. There was just enough room for the two of us to sit down beside a pile of *Post-Dispatch*es. I put Justin's wallet on top of the pile. The outside was covered with gutter scum but the inside was in good shape. It was the kind of wallet that had sections with snaps. The first one we opened had cards with his name showing he belonged to the Knights of Columbus, the Shriners, the Elks, and the Salvation Army.

The next compartment was fat with money, mostly fifty-dollar bills. I had never seen anything higher than a twenty, and not many of those. I didn't know a fifty-dollar bill even existed. Augie jumped up and did a little kind of hop dance.

"Boy oh boy oh boy!" he said, quietly riffling the bills. "We're rich, Aaron, we're rich!"

I grabbed his shirt and pulled him down. "What do you mean, we're rich?"

"We add it up, split it fifty-fifty, and get rid of the wallet. Just look at all those fifties and twenties!"

"It's not our money."

"You mean let him keep it?"

"Course."

"You ever heard of the law—finders keepers?"

"That's when you don't know the owner."

"He'll never miss it and for us it's to live on."

"He may give us a reward—you can live on that."

"You poor sap. You have no idea how things work do you?"

"Maybe not, but I know what's honest and what's not. I'm no Boy Scout—if it's to get life-or-death medicine that's one thing. But when it's to *steal . . .*"

Augie split the money and put his half in his pocket. "Call it what you want. You can put your part back in the wallet and show him what a good little boy you are. All I ask is you say this is the way you found it."

"And if he doesn't believe me? If he gets tough with me, what then?"

"Okay, let's just put it back in the gutter."

"Without the money you just took?"

"Yup. I'm sure he doesn't know how much—"

"Augie, listen, my father's not much of a thinker and what he believes in are pretty simple, corny things, and one of them is honesty is the best policy."

"You're living in a ratty Hooverville, you've got, what? Ten cents in your pocket?"

"Seventy-four."

"You don't know where your next meal is coming from."

"But my soul is okay."

"So? What's your soul got to do with it?"

"My soul is who I am. I want to keep it as it is. How about you? You think about your soul?"

Augie closed his eyes and I guess thought about his soul. He thought about it for quite some time.

"It is the one thing the Depression can't take from us long as we take care of it," I said. "I have this thing about my soul. First I heard of it was when I saw a kid in a movie with his pajamas on kneel down at his bed, prayer up his hands, and say, as best I remember: 'Now I lay me down to sleep and pray the Lord my soul to keep, but if I die before I wake, I pray the Lord my soul to take.' I thought the part about a six-year-old kid dying in his sleep was pretty silly, but the soul part of it got me thinking and I spent a long time thinking about my soul, that it's the good part of me, that it can keep me going or leave me empty. I will definitely not hurt my soul for a fistful of Justin's fifties."

Augie finally opened his eyes, took the money from his pocket, put it back in the wallet.

I opened the next section of the wallet, mostly receipts and business cards and junk like that, but Augie held up a small white card that had

writing on it: Catfish Dannemora and a telephone number. Attached to it with a paper clip
was a telephone number with the initials G.A.T.

"What do you know," he said. "Looka that."

I looked but drew a blank. "What about it?"

"Catfish—you don't know about Catfish?"

"No. Why should I?"

"Catfish Kuger?"

"Who's he?"

"Jeez, it's not *that* long ago. The Kuger gang,
the Memorial Day Massacre on Market Street?"

"It says Dannemora—who's he?"

"Oh boy! It's not a he—it's a max-security
prison in New York where a Fed judge put him
for life to keep him away from St. Louis but the
Post says he has cronies here who run his gambling boats and his other stuff."

"There's that telephone number. He's got a
private phone?"

Augie got a laugh out of that. "No, that's probably the number of the warden. But the other
telephone number with G.A.T., that's the one
might tell us something."

"Let's give it a try."

"Why don't we go to the *Post-Dispatch* and
look it up before we phone."

"What could it tell us?"

"Pictures. Can't tell who we might see."

"Like G.A.T.?"

"Yeah."

"Here, Augie, you give Justin the wallet—maybe he'll give you a good reward. As Hilda Levy said, 'You can never tell when to expect the unexpected.'"

"Sure, he's gonna say, 'Keep the cash, kid, honesty is the best policy.'"

I had it wrong about the chili: It was chili con *corny* in Ella's note not carne. Corn was a St. Louis summer plenty, yellow and white, the fields thick with it, the farmer's co-op on St. Louis plaza even giving it to the needy and most of us qualified. But I want you to know that sitting outside their shack on boxes, eating the chili off tin plates, was as good as any chili with carne I ever had. Ella's mom was a home-run cook, no two ways about it. A can of beans, an onion, corn off the cob to come out like that!

Afterward Ella and I took the plates to the Hooverville wash station where water was pumped in from the Mississippi. There was also a faucet for drinking water that came from a city pipe. Farther on were a couple of stalls, one marked men the other women, where you could have a shower but you had to have your own towel and soap. Ella had given me a towel and a hunk of soap that I kept hidden with my bottle of water.

She cranked up her Victrola and, sitting on the outside boxes, we listened to Louis Armstrong while Mrs. McShane wrote letters by the light of her kerosene lamp. Ella's hair was piled up in a sort of bun and she was wearing a dress, instead of her usual pants, and some lipstick. For the first time she seemed a little like a woman, not a girl. I never did know her age, maybe fifteen or sixteen.

I asked her what I had planned to ask her— would she help me interview Bonnie Porter who was such a lady, wears swell clothes, and isn't like the saleswomen in the Scruggs department store.

"In fact," I said, "everyone in the J & J is turning out to be different from what they seem to be. I thought maybe we'd pretend you were writing about the murder for the *Globe-Democrat* and you were interviewing everyone who saw it. I'd like to be with you, maybe the photographer if your mom can lend me her box camera. I wouldn't need film, but am I too young?"

"Of course you are, but you could be my assistant and hand me the camera, something like that. She's married to the actor Roy Delray so I guess she likes publicity."

"The *Globe-Democrat* is second fiddle to the

Post-Dispatch but I agree, beautiful people who wear beautiful things like to have their picture taken."

Ella said she'd phone her in the morning from the nickel phone on the corner and set a time for us to interview her.

I asked her to look as grown up as possible. "Your hair, maybe one of your mom's dresses, and beads, no lipstick."

"Why, Aaron! You know a lot about women, don't you?"

I blushed.

Happening 24

When Augie said we were going to the *Post-Dispatch* morgue to find out about Catfish Kuger I expected something spooky, but the morgue was just a bright-lit room in the *Post-Dispatch* building with long tables and chairs and rows upon rows of files all around the room with moving ladders on rollers to reach the files on top.

Augie filled out a paper for the woman at the desk and she brought the Catfish Kuger file to the desk where we were sitting. The file was chock-full of clippings and photos. We skipped through the early stuff about the event—Catfish and his men machine-gunning the eight guys of the Chicago Collazo gang that was trying to move in on him. And then came the bundle of photos. Augie had brought his father's magnifying glass and that was a big help since some of the photos were kind of grainy. We both let out a whoop when a clear photo of Catfish turned up: A dapper guy he was with a pencil mustache and classy clothes, holding on to the arm of Matt J. Pringle, but his name under the photo wasn't Pringle, it was Anthony Aravista, a lawyer, the article said, who'd been disbarred, which was a word I didn't know but I guessed it meant he'd been busted. His face was a little different—probably he'd had it monkeyed with—but it was Pringle all right. There was a woman on the other side of Catfish who was holding his hand. Her face looked a little familiar but it was half hidden and not clear enough to really see it.

"What do you think?" Augie said.

"I think Catfish is all over J & J," I said. "Ella and I are going to interview Bonnie, so maybe you and I ought to have a talk with Grace Dorso."

"Are you sure about the watch-repair guy?"

"Shucks no, not now. One thing I am sure of— my poor father's been caught up in something that has nothing to do with Bulova watches. I keep remembering what we heard the J & J brothers saying that time at Pete's. And Justin being tossed in the gutter. I sure have learned not to make up my mind about people and things I haven't seen and heard with my own two eyes and ears. Things that you think are real are really make-believe that can hide something that can kill you. That's how it was with

Mr. Sherlock Holmes—he could sniff out the true from the false. I guess if he were here by now he'd know who killed Dempsey and my pop would be out of jail. I just gotta do what Sherlock would do and it'll happen as long as I can stay clear of Freda Muller."

Augie said he would do his part with Pringle, follow him and try to find out his connection with the Catfish people. The newspaper articles we were reading said Catfish was still able to control dockworkers on the Mississippi, gambling boats, and protection for businesses. Neither Augie nor I knew what "protection" meant but we could tell it wasn't a good thing that he was able to do all this while serving a life sentence in Dannemora prison!

The more I thought about this, the more I feared I'd never be able to get my father out of the trap he was in. And that I'd be able to spring him with my brilliant detectifying was just the babble of a kid who had read a couple of Sherlock Holmes books. So far, all I was doing was stirring the pot but not producing anything to chew on. And maybe the Catfish people or Freda Muller were going to get me long before I could get them.

We were out on the sidewalk now and I said,

"Augie, would you please give me a swift kick in the butt?"

"What?"

"I'm coming apart and I need a jolt."

"And you're giving up on your pop?"

"No, on me."

"You don't need a kick in the butt. You're starving that's all. It's time we divvy up the big reward I got when I gave Justin his wallet— a pat on my head and 'Thanks kid' as he handed me a dollar from his pile of money. Come on, you don't need a kick, you need a hamburger."

We were passing a White Castle and we both had a hamburger with all the works and a Nehi soda. Grape. That's the first and only time I was on the verge of giving up.

Augie raised his Nehi and I raised mine.

"E pluribus unum," he said.

"What?"

"E pluribus unum."

"What does that mean?"

"I don't know. My pop says it and it sounds good."

"All right. E pluribus . . ."

"Unum."

We clicked our Nehis.

Ella was waiting outside her shack when I came to get her for our meeting with Bonnie Porter. At first I didn't recognize Ella the way she had fixed herself up to look like a grown-up reporter for the *Globe*. She sure looked the part. She handed me an empty box camera that belonged to her mother that I was to carry and hand to her as her assistant. She had a red notepad and a pen in a bag she carried over her shoulder.

Bonnie lived with her husband, Roy Delray, in a small neat house on Carondelet Avenue. Ella said that when she phoned her Bonnie seemed eager to be interviewed by the *Globe*. Like most beautiful women, Ella said, Bonnie wants to be noticed.

She certainly was all smiles and welcome when she opened the door to our ring. She was spiffed up for the interview, her long blond hair curly around her beautiful face, a blue silk dress with matching shoes.

She seated us in the living room facing the fireplace where there was an oil painting of her on the wall above it and a large photo of a fierce-looking Veiled Prophet on the mantel. Next to the fireplace there was a piano with many more photos on it. The one that caught my eye showed a Veiled Prophet armed with jeweled daggers and golden pistols attached to his silky robe that billowed to the ground. His getup was topped by a high conical decorated hood and a long heavy veil you could not see through. He was dancing with a gorgeous Queen of Love and Beauty, who was Bonnie. She saw me fixated on the photo.

"That's when I was Queen of Love and Beauty at the Veiled Prophet Ball," she said. "That was the year I was a debutante and I was chosen by the Veiled Prophet from among all the debutantes to be the Queen. My picture was everywhere."

"Who was the Veiled Prophet that year?" Ella asked, her pad and pencil ready.

"No one knows. All those Veiled Prophets since the very beginning in 1870-something, not one of their names has ever been revealed."

"You mean you didn't know who selected you? Who you were dancing with?" Ella asked. She made notes in her pad.

"No idea. The Veiled Prophet's makeup has

always been so spectacular, well, I could have been dancing with my own father and I wouldn't have known it."

I knew about the Veiled Prophet, the Queen, and all that. I had been going with my mother to the Veiled Prophet parades on the riverfront since I was four or five years old, the fancy floats and marching bands and candies thrown to us kids by the people on the floats. There was also the fun some peashooters had, pelting those hoity-toities on the floats.

My mother told me the whole Veiled Prophet thing was started by a St. Louis gentleman of high society who had copied it from a Mardi Gras celebration he had witnessed in New Orleans. My mother knew a lot about the Veiled Prophet Society and the Veiled Prophet Ball that was St. Louis's big social event every year. She told me the name came from the Irish poet Thomas Moore and his Veiled Prophet of Khorassan. It was a secret society of the rich.

"Although no one has ever revealed the name of a Veiled Prophet," Bonnie was saying, "I do know one and I can reveal it to you if you keep it strictly off the record. Promise?"

"Of course," Ella said. She was absolutely

being a really good reporter. She closed her note-pad and put her pen down.

"My father," Bonnie said. "Benjamin Quincy Porter. He was Veiled Prophet ten years or so before I was Queen."

"Is he the Porter of Porter Chemicals?" Ella asked.

"He is," Bonnie said.

"And the Porter Chemical Building?"

"Yes."

"So tell me, being who you are why are you a salesperson behind the counter at J & J?"

"Well that's a sad story. In a nutshell, I fell in love with the actor Roy Delray. You know of him?"

"Yes," Ella said, "he does the Mississippi Music Program on KMOX."

"And the Muny in the park. My father was very opposed to my marrying him, threatening to disown me. Bringing an actor into our family was like a scourge, an incurable disease that would poison the pure Porter name, said he would positively disown me . . . and he did— that was four years ago, he pitched me out of our beautiful house in Clayton and I haven't heard from him or seen him since. Not even a Christmas card. The Depression hasn't touched him or his big chemical business but it sure touched us. You ask why this Queen of Love and Beauty is working at J & J, it's for Roy and me to keep afloat. He doesn't make much singing and acting on KMOX and the Muny, which is owned by the city. It pays little but added to my puny salary we get by. We eat out and go to movies and we like to dance on the Mississippi steamboat *River Princess*, where Roy gets a booking once in a while to sing in the gambling lounge."

"Do you regret your fall-out with your father?" Ella asked.

"And lose Roy? No, of course not, no, no, no."

"Is there anyone at J & J or any little thing that happened that you think might lead to finding out who was in cahoots with the shooter? Any little suspicion?"

"I've thought about it a lot—I really and truly liked Dempsey, the nicest, kindest man—but I haven't come up with a thing. I don't socialize with anyone there."

"Well, thank you for your time," Ella said, putting her pad and pencil away.

"Before you go may I offer you tea and a slice of my very own pound cake? It's the one really positive thing about getting booted from the family—I have discovered I'm quite a good baker. Roy says I should open a bakery."

Her pound cake certainly was delicious. She kept putting slices on my plate and I kept devouring them.

"I agree with Roy," I said, my mouth full.

"He's performing at the Muny in Shakespeare's *The Merry Wives of Windsor*. Would you two like to go see him? I have some house seats."

"Oh, yes," I said. "Could we have one more? We have a friend at the *Globe* who I'm sure would like to come with us."

"Oh, of course," she said, handing me three tickets. "When will this article appear?"

"Never can tell," Ella said. "It's up to the editor."

I handed her the camera and she clicked Bonnie posing all over the room, at the piano and so forth, Ella clicking away like she knew what she was doing.

"You need any more pictures, especially with Roy," Bonnie said, "I'd be happy to oblige."

Happening 26

Ella and I took the trolley to the Eads Bridge stop and parted company at the door of her shack. She hugged me goodbye and I complimented her on being such a good actress.

I was halfway to my hammock when my arm was grabbed. "Hey, kid, looka me, I got a message for you." He was a short, wide man with a heavy mustache and huge muscley arms with tattooed serpents sticking out of his shirt with the sleeves cut off.

"You been sticking your nose where it don't belong and there are people don't like it, so the message is . . . back off. We don't wanna see you hanging around anymore or your skinny little ass is going to be busted. You got that?" He shifted his muscley grip from my arm to the shirt around my throat, pulling me up off the ground, and I started to choke. I tried to talk but only a smothered squeak came out. I tried to breathe but I couldn't draw any air into me. I wanted to bite his hand but it wasn't close enough to my mouth. I pulled at his hand but it was like trying to move a cement sidewalk. I began to feel dizzy, maybe collapse when he suddenly let go. He put his face right up against mine.

"Don't let me see you again."

I nodded.

"Understand?"

I nodded.

He left.

I sat down on the ground, massaged my throat, tested my voice, which was still kind of squeaky. I tried to unscramble what he said to figure out who could have sicced him on me.

After a few minutes resting on the ground I began to feel better. I managed to force myself up and test my shaky legs. They seemed to be in working order and able to take me to the hammock. But the prospect of a soothing swing in the hammock was undone by the sight of a body occupying it.

My first panicked reaction was that Captain Arnold had returned and was geared to finish what mighty muscles had started. My instinct was to turn tail and get out of there, but I just kept going toward the hammock and when I got there Captain Arnold turned out to be Augie.

"Augie! What the devil are you doing here? How'd you find me?"

"You're the only hammock in all of Hooverville, that's how."

He swung himself out of the hammock and I staggered into his place.

"Geez, Aaron, you look like a ghost got hold of you."

"Yeah a muscley ghost with serpents on his arms tried to get rid of me."

"One of Catfish's thugs, you think?"

"Yeah. Why you here?"

"I was tailing Pringle from work and guess who he went to visit?"

"The Marmon flapper."

"Nope. Grace Dorso."

"Chubby Grace? Are they all in cahoots?"

"She lives in a swell ground-floor apartment at Lindell Towers. I got under an open window and I heard them talking. They certainly know each other pretty good. He had something to give her—don't know what—I couldn't stay there long, there were people coming and going, but I did see them come out and from what I heard he was taking her to dinner."

"We know Pringle is all wound up with Catfish, but what about Grace?"

"I think we should get on over there and take a look in her apartment."

"You mean break in?"

"The window's open so we wouldn't break in, just *step* in—couldn't be easier. Zip in, zip out."

What suddenly zipped into me was that terrible pain of the thug's grip on my arm and it began to be hard to breathe. I swung out of the hammock, not wanting Augie to see me sprouting fear. Of course I'll go! You bet I'll go! I said to myself. So what if we get caught. So what? Are you some kind of wimp, weasel, worm, afraid of your own shadow?

"What the hell's wrong with you?" Augie said.

"Whatcha mean? Nothing's wrong."

"Then why are you punching the air and swinging your arms?"

"Come on! Let's go and get it over with!" I said.

I was breathing better but my neck felt like one of those serpents was wound around it, squeezing.

Lindell Towers was a large apartment building close to a busy entrance to Forest Park. Grace Dorso's ground-floor apartment was in the rear where there was less Forest Park people traffic. We waited for a lull until we boosted ourselves into the apartment. In addition to my neck hurting, I was feeling bad because I mostly lived by the rules and although I take chances not big ones like this. Of course everything I do right now is to help my father but if I get into trouble, who's there to replace me looking after him?

It was a small apartment but the furniture and curtains and rugs and pictures looked expensive. Augie led the way into the living room. I looked around, no idea what I was looking for. Augie began to open the drawers of a mirrored desk and I went over to a table where there was a clutch of framed photographs, mostly people at parties and faded photos of what must have been family.

Augie held up an account book he had found in one of the desk drawers. "It's for that gambling boat, the *River Princess*, all these names and dollar amounts and look at this—Roy Delray with a big number."

"Bonnie said he sometimes worked the floor show. Maybe that's what he got paid."

"But what's it doing in Grace's desk? Maybe it's for something else."

"I'll be darned! Look at this photo," I said.

It was a young couple in wedding dress and tuxedo. The woman looked vaguely familiar but the man was definitely the Catfish we saw at the *Post-Dispatch* morgue.

"The woman," Augie said, "why would Grace have the photo in this super-fancy frame?"

"Looks to me . . . maybe a sister?"

"Yeah, skinny, pretty sister or . . ."

I was studying the photo, holding it in the window light, turning it this way and that.

"You know something," I said. "Tell you what. She's beefed herself up, and done a ton to her face, but you know something—that's Grace back then."

"Naw I don't see it. Maybe a sister, yes, but . . ."

I turned the photo around, took off the backing, and there was a folded marriage certificate

with two names: Gaetano Cugavelo and Graciella Borsolini, Gaetano to become Catfish and
after being put in Dannemora for life, Graciella
changes her name and her face and fattens up to
become pudgy Grace Dorso.

"You think Catfish still runs his outfit outa
Dannemora through Grace?" Augie asked.

I was replacing the picture's backing and putting it back on the table. "And through Pringle.
She probably takes the train every month to visit
Catfish and he passes to her what Pringle needs
to do."

"And they run the whole thing through J & J."

"Yeah, and those diamonds that were swiped
from the case probably belong to Catfish."

"The whole thing as tangled as a bowl of spaghetti. You're A-OK, Aaron. You've really got it
going."

"But I don't see how any of it will help me
catch the killer and get my poor father out of the
clink. I don't have much time. Last night I had
horrible nightmares with Freda Muller chasing
me all over Forest Park."

The sharp sound of a key unlocking the door
sent us flying toward the open window. Augie
dived out headfirst and so did I, landing right on
top of him. A noisy group of teenagers were sing-

ing and dancing on their way to the park and we quickly joined up with them. A very pretty girl grabbed my arm and offered me a swig of her bottle of beer. I don't much like the taste of beer or any of that gunk but I like pretty girls so I took a swallow and sort of danced with her all the way to the park. They had a basket of peanut butter sandwiches and tamales and we sat in a circle and sang songs and watched the moon come up.

Happening 28

Sitting in the tenth row at the eleven-thousand-seat Muny instead of the free seats at the very top when I went with my mom was like the difference between very hot and ice cold. Ella, Augie, and I were handed printed programs and ushered to our seats. Eleven thousand is a really lot of seats and they filled one entire hillside of the park. I looked back over the huge number of people slanted up behind me and felt kind of special, a way I hadn't felt for a long, long time.

We turned the pages of our programs. Up front was *The Merry Wives of Windsor* by William Shakespeare, followed by the cast of characters. At the top was Sir John Falstaff...Roy Delray, followed by a long cast. On separate pages marked Meet the Actors, there were real-life pictures of the actors, not in costume, and short biographies. There was a picture of Roy Delray in a spiffy suit and necktie, slim, very handsome, looking sort of like the movie star Ronald Colman.

There were musicians in the pit in front of the stage but this wasn't a musical so I guessed they were there to play backup while the actors spoke their parts. The music was playing now as the audience came to their seats and I could feel the air of excitement that gets stirred up at the start of all theater I've seen.

It was dark now and the stage lights came alive, the audience applauded (the three of us included) as the players in fancy Elizabethan costumes began to come onstage. Big fat bloated Falstaff entered with a jeweled sword at his side, a giant buckle above his huge legs, boots up to his knees, a mountain of a belly, and his fat body covered with gaudy robes, plus a stout beard and a whopping halo of hair. When he spoke his voice was heavy and rumbly.

Ella and I looked at each other. It was hard to believe that this actor was the man we had seen on Bonnie's piano or the one in the program. Or in the scene where Falstaff disguises himself as the wise woman of Bradford, a mountain of a woman in a colorful billowing dress, her fat legs bouncing off each other as she waddled across the stage.

At the finale the audience gave the cast a big ovation with lots of bows and special bravos and whistles for Falstaff. Roy had fumbled his lines and his accent a couple of times but it didn't seem to matter to the audience.

AFTER WE filed out of the Muny, Augie suggested we all go to the park's pavilion for root beers, "On me—I did pretty good today." I said no because I said I had some things I had to attend to. The zoo with its animal sounds was not far away and I headed in that direction. I knew it really well. At the Westgate Hotel I often escaped the severe heat of our room, my parents' angry quarrels, the loud music of the Good Times ten-cents-a-dance hall with its three-piece band, by making my way to the zoo. I spent most of my time outside the cages of the big cats and developed a good pal-ship with an old lion named Fritz who had a black mane and soulful eyes.

When I got to the zoo I sat down on a bench under a lamp and started to write things down in my notebook. It was time to do some honest-to-God detectifying, to put two and two together the way Mr. Holmes did and Miss Marple did and Inspector Poirot.

My mind was going this way and that, revisiting events and conversations: the tangle of Justin and Joel, Catfish Kuger, Pringle who was really Anthony Aravista, Pete's, Bonnie and her big-shot father, Grace Dorso who was really Graciella Borsolini married to Catfish, the Marmon flapper, Sol Greenblatt and his bunch of ex-jeweler poker players, Roy Delray waddling around the stage, all that mysterious stuff about the Veiled Prophet.

After scribbling for a while, trying to work things out, my stomach began to growl, the way it does when I put off eating to save my fading money, but from the way it was growling and carrying on this was definitely a time to dip into my leaky treasury. I went over to Fritz's cage and he came over to see me. I talked to him and he sent a few purrs my way.

There was a bus stop just outside the zoo and I grabbed a bus to Gino's, that little restaurant in Dago Hill where a steaming five-cent plate of their spaghetti will certainly answer my stomach's call.

I SAT DOWN at the counter and two slices of warm Italian bread were put on my plate while I waited for the spaghetti. The restaurant's tables were lively and pretty full.

I had just taken a bite out of the warm, crusty bread when the door banged open and a tall man with a cap pulled down to his eyes and a gun in his hand came in and went straight to the counter. I choked on my bread, positive he was in cahoots with the guy who grabbed me at the Hooverville and was coming to finish me off, but he walked right by me and aimed his gun at a man sitting at the other end of the counter who was yelling, "No, Joe! No, Joe!" But Joe shot the man who fell from his chair with blood oozing out of him. A man at one of the tables stood up with a gun in his hand and fired two quick shots at the shooter who spun around and dropped to the floor two seats away from me. The whole restaurant was now in an uproar, guns came out all over the place. All I knew was to get out of there fast before the police came. My heart was thumping something awful and I had trouble getting my legs to move with two dead men in my way. Sirens were already in the air and there was a mob of eaters pushing and pulling to get out the front door, probably types who were better off not having to deal with the cops.

I somehow managed to squirm my way out

the door and onto the sidewalk, getting myself as far as the corner when the first police cars sirened up. It wasn't until I got on the trolley and showed my pass that I noticed my hand was clutching the pieces of bread from my plate, so I didn't have to go to sleep on an empty stomach after all.

Happening 29

My sleep that night was overrun with night-mares, blazing guns and spurting blood, hard-fisted killers chasing me from one end of the Muny to the other with me jumping over the seats and the hammock pitching as if in a hurricane.

I woke when the sun turned on its St. Louis furnace. I took my towel and soap from its hiding place and went to the showers. The cold water gave my hot body a real good boost as I tried to wash away the night's misery with an extra-good soaping.

Outside the Hooverville I stopped for a slice of toast and a glass of milk and looked at the to-do list that I had written in my notepad. First off was a visit to Scruggs Vandervort and Barney. I saw Augie busy at his corner and went to talk to him.

"What's doing, Aaron?"

"Checking out some things at Scruggs. How'd you like the show?"

"Well, honestly, I'm not much into Shakespeare. But I sure liked meeting Ella. She's neat, isn't she?"

"You bet she is."

"We got along just great. She has a wonderful voice. You ever hear her sing? I'm going to see her again on Friday."

"Swell."

"Told me about her epilepsy."

"She has a medicine for it."

"Doesn't matter. We've all got something," Augie said.

IT'S NOT easy finding your way around Scruggs but with help I found the departments I was looking for—leisure clothes, hats, gloves. Not to buy anything, of course, I was just looking for information.

After Scruggs I went to the headquarters of the Veiled Prophet Society. I pushed the outside button and received a response from the squawk box.

"Password please."

"I don't know it, but——"

"Are you a member?"

"No. I just want to talk to your costume and makeup people."

"Sorry, we are a secret society and we do not divulge anything."

"Yes, sir, I know but I'm going to a costume party and I just want to find out from your costume——"

"Only members have access to our costume people. We don't disclose anything to anyone who isn't a member of the Veiled Prophet Society." With that, he turned off the squawk box.

I HAD much better luck with the Muny because it was owned and run by St. Louis. The wardrobe mistress walked me around all the costumes which filled a special building, rows and rows and rows of everything you could imagine from pirates to cowboys to kings, princes, queens, jesters, knights in armor, Gypsies, generals, cops, monsters, animals, doctors, judges, and on and on and on.

I said, "I guess costumes are being borrowed all the time, aren't they?"

"Not anymore," she said. "A lot of our cos-

tumes went missing, borrowed and never returned, so a few years ago all these costumes
were attached and can only be released by me
and my master key. No costume has gone missing since then."

The makeup keeper was just as nice as the
wardrobe lady, showing me drawer after drawer
of noses, ears, eyes, feet, hands, chins (double
and sunken), beards, necks, foreheads, legs,
hunchbacks, endless stuff all in drawers under
lock and key.

AS LONG AS I was in the park, I decided to go
to the tennis courts where I knew people and felt
comfortable. There were picnic tables outside
the Drop Shot where I could sit and look over
the pages of my notebook and do some serious
detectifying. The pages went all the way back
to when I was trapped in the Ford, watching the
cops take my father away. But the only pages I
wanted to deal with now were the ones about the
J & J people, Catfish and his gang, everything
that happened that had anything to do with
the diamonds stolen from the J & J glass case.
I thought about all this very hard. I don't know
if you can hurt your brain with overthinking,

like when a candle burns out way before its time because the wick is much too big.

So with my head crammed to overflowing, I know the time has come to do *something* to free my father, and I've made up my mind as to what I can possibly do, and if right now is the time to do it.

I was closing up my notepad and putting it in my back pocket when Buddy Silverstone called to me from the Drop Shot.

"Hey, Aaron, come help me carry."

I went over to where Buddy was fixing two trays with plates of hot dogs in buns and mounds of baked beans plus glasses of lemonade.

"My birthday today," Buddy said, "and I'd like you to celebrate with me."

Buddy was an old guy, fifty or something, with a short neat beard and muddled black-and-white hair. He had a riotous laugh that burst out of him and caused many a double fault; he was convinced that everyone should be having some fun, no matter what. Perfect guy to run the tennis courts. He had the beginning of a potbelly but he still played nifty doubles.

"I gave your hot dog the Silverstone works," he said. "Mustard, ketchup, relish, and fried onions. Also Tabasco in the beans."

"Boy oh boy, happy birthday, Buddy," I said, my mouth peppery from the Tabasco.

"The fried onions are my invention," Buddy said. "I made one for the Cardinals' food guy at Sportsman's Park and he said he's listed it on the menu board as a Buddy Dog." He roared his laugh, causing a player on the nearby court to whiff on an overhead.

"Haven't seen you around much, Aaron. Something wrong? I know about your mom, but besides?"

I told him about my father and the Ford and getting locked out while I was mopping up the juice of the beans with the heel of my bun.

"You mean you're living out of a hammock in the Eads Bridge Hooverville?"

"Really not bad, showers and everything."

"Sure and a laundry and electricity and a grocery and a refrigerator," he said sarcastically. "Look, Aaron, all the years you've played here, I've seen what a great kid you are. If you had some lessons you could play competitive tennis, the tournaments. Tim would swap you his pro lessons for your book reports—he's at Washington University and his grades need help. What about it? It's time you had fun like a kid your age should have."

I told him how much it meant that he cared about me, especially in a bad stretch like this. But there were a lot of kids like me having to take their lumps and either you ride out the storm or you get swept up and drowned. "It's great to have someone like you around, ready with a life preserver. The ship is taking on water but I'm bailing fast as I can. I have resilliance."

"Resilience."

"Right. I have a lot of that."

"Good, but don't confuse movement with action."

So I decided all my running around, interviewing, breaking in, and all that was ready to be put into action. I got permission from Buddy to make a local call on his tennis-court phone. I fished the lawyer card out of my pocket to find the number for Lawyer Appleton. His secretary answered.

"This is Aaron Broom," I said, trying to sound grown-up, "may I please talk to Mr. Appleton." I felt good saying "may" instead of "can" as Hilda Levy had taught us.

"He's with a client right now but please give me your number and he'll return your call."

Just hearing her say "return your call" made me feel like I was somebody. I gave her the tennis-court number. Then I sat down next to the phone which was on a glass counter that sold sweatbands, Spalding balls, tennis shirts and caps with St. Louis logos, and socks. Tim Storch, the tennis pro, came over and asked whether I'd like to hit some with a player who was looking for a partner. Tim offered to lend me a racket.

I did, and it felt wonderful stretching my legs and hitting full out on both forehands and backhands.

When the call came from Lawyer Appleton I was pretty sweaty. "I've been working hard Mr. Appleton and I'd like to tell you about it—I hope it's enough for you to maybe get my father out of jail."

"Well, Mr. Broom, I'm pretty tied up tomorrow, but perhaps at the end of the day . . . how's five o'clock?"

"Oh, that would be peachy. Thanks so much."

I was really amazed that he would see me and so quickly. I feared that maybe the time before he was just being nice to me, a needy kid off the street, but giving me this appointment really lifted me way up.

I WENT to Augie's corner to share the good news but he wasn't there. An older kid had taken his place.

"Where's Augie?"

"Dunno."

"Is he sick or something?"

"Dunno."

"You know where he lives?"

He picked up a *Post-Dispatch* sales book from the newsstand and handed it to me. On the cover was Augie's name and address.

"You can keep it," the new kid said. "I got one of my own."

"You mean he's been fired?"

"Dunno."

"What *do* you know?"

"He's gone."

"For good?"

"Dunno."

I felt a rise of something like panic. In this short time Augie had become an honest-to-God buddy, someone I could count on and he on me. I felt in my bones that something had struck him down.

It was an address on Union Boulevard, a large squat building, apartment 3R. The door was half open. There was no sound from within. I pushed the door button and a ring sounded.

"Yeah?"

"It's me, Augie—Aaron. Can I come in?"

"Sure, oh, sure, A. I'm in the bedroom."

It was a small affair, bedroom, living room, kitchen, and bathroom. Augie was putting his things into an open suitcase on the bed.

"Augie! What the dickens this? Where you going?"

He stopped packing, took my arm and led me into the living room where we both sat down on the couch.

"My bed," he said, punching up the pillows.

He was having a hard time so I just sat quietly and let him travel through his feelings. He went to the kitchen and got us two glasses of water. I wasn't in a mood to drink. He sipped at his.

"I came home yesterday and found my father sitting in that chair over there. He had a package in his lap with my name on it. I talked to him: 'Something for me?' He didn't answer. I touched him and he leaned to one side. The package fell on the floor. He was dead."

My body went cold all over, and my breath backed up on me. I felt guilty. I wanted to say something but this was not a time for words. We just sat there, the two of us, sharing the pain. Augie had his head cupped in his hands. There were outside sounds of passing cars and street-cars and people. The life that would go on but Augie's father would no longer be a part of it now and Augie would have to live with a hole in his heart.

Augie raised his head and said, "He left me a note attached to a beautiful broach with diamonds and rubies." He opened the box, took out the note, and read: "This is the last piece of your mother's jewelry. Her jewelry box is now empty. We are down to our last few dollars but I can't bear to sell it, and then what? Out on the street, me back on the curb with all the other apple sellers, begging, us trying to get by on the few pennies you earn. So I leave you this beautiful broach which should provide you with enough to get along for a while. I've spoken to my cousin Leonard in Keokuk and he has agreed to take you in and maybe find you some kind of work. Please go back to school soon as you can. You are a noble and intelligent boy destined to go places. Marry well and if you should have the good fortune of having a son please name him after me so I can continue to love you and be a part of your family." Augie put the broach back in the box.

I had tears in my eyes. "A wonderful man, Augie, so full of love. What are your plans?"

"I thought about staying and helping you out with your dad, but after tomorrow I think it's best I get out of here."

"What's tomorrow?"

"The funeral. My dad belonged to a funeral society so it's all paid for—the transfer, the casket, the McKinley Funeral Parlor, the cremation," suddenly shouting, "all that shit!" He was embarrassed. "I'm not handling this very well."

"How about we hang out tonight?"

"I'd like to but I have lots of stuff to tend to. The apartment's furnished but there's his clothes and a few books and stuff like that."

"You keeping anything?"

"No. It all has the stink of giving up, but there's something you can do for me."

"Sure. Anything."

"Come to McKinley's tomorrow. I'd rather not be there by myself."

"Of course I'll come. Mind if I bring a few people . . . like Ella and her mom?"

He perked up a bit at that. "Sure, I'd like to say goodbye to her."

He picked up the package his father had left him, opened it, taking out its contents: the family Bible, a bus ticket to Keokuk, six one-dollar bills, cuff links, a compass, a silver fountain pen, a bundle of letters from his mother, opera glasses, wristwatch, and the beautiful broach. He took them into the bedroom and packed them carefully in his suitcase except for the six dollars which he put in his pocket.

"I don't know about moving in with this cousin. I never met him, in fact, never heard of him. I guess he has a family. I'm not really up to all that." He took a long, thinking pause. "I'll probably be better off on my own, starting with the six dollars."

WALKING DOWN the stairs from Augie's place I felt terrible, like I was deserting him. Even though he wanted to be alone, I still felt I should have stayed with him, not walked away, down these stairs. I myself was alone for the time being so I sort of knew the feeling but I had a mother and a father who were still in my life only not for now.

But Augie had been suddenly cast adrift, in a terribly sad way. Finding his father dead in a chair like that. Feeling now that he had to get away from this bad-luck life but totally unsure that Keokuk was the place to drop anchor, either with or without his cousin.

When I showed up at the door of Ella's shack-tent there was a mouthwatering aroma in the air. Ella came to the door and asked me in. She and her mom were making corn bread in a skillet, cooking over a flame from a Sterno can. I apologized for disturbing them.

"Can you imagine," Ella said. "I went to the hardware store down the block to buy a can of Sterno and when I got there the owner was putting an 'Out of Business' sign on the door. He gave me all his Sterno cans for five cents, the price of one can. 'Nobody buys anything,' he said, 'so what's the use?' My God how the world's gone sad."

Mrs. McShane cut a corner piece of the corn bread from the skillet for me to taste.

"You're right, Ella, the world is a really sad place." I then told them the terrible fate of Augie and his father and how Augie had a bus ticket to

Keokuk after the funeral and would they please come to McKinley's the next day for his sake.

"He found his father like that?" Ella said, her voice breaking as she bent her head and hooded her eyes with her hands. Her mother came over and hugged me and said, "Of course we'll come."

Ella looked up, wiping at her tears. "Is Augie all right?" she asked.

"He'll be glad to see you," I said.

IT WAS a long shot to find the boys who were baking those potatoes in that drum. I finally did find the drum but it was not fired up and no one was around. I figured, though, that the boys must be from shacks nearby. I went door to door knocking on shacks in the vicinity and one knock paid off when the boy named Frank, who was the nice one who gave me the potato, answered the door.

"Remember me?" I said.

"Sure, you're the kid that drop-kicked big Jim in the balls."

"Is he all right?"

"Oh, sure." He laughed. "It straightened him out."

I told him about Augie and the funeral and asked if he would come and bring somebody. "I know it's pushy of me to ask," I said, "since he's a stranger, but he's a really good guy who shouldn't have to bury his dad without some people with him in the room with the casket."

"My pop got killed in the war and me and my mom never had the chance to bury him, so I'm glad to be able to be there for your friend."

AUGIE CAME early and he was pleased to greet Ella and her mother when they arrived. It was a small room, the open coffin in front. There was canned organ music playing soft chords.

Frank showed up and to my good surprise brought Roger and big Jim, the potato-drum threesome. I introduced them to Augie and to Ella and Mrs. McShane. Big Jim made it a point of being friendly with me which is what Vernon had predicted about bullies. "Knock 'em down they'll get up lickin' your boots."

Watching through the window, I saw Vernon arrive with Arthur. I went outside to join them on the sidewalk. They were both dressed up neat with neckties. I opened the door and they followed me in. As we approached the room where Augie was, a tall man slickly dressed in a black suit, white shirt, black tie, a handkerchief with three points in his breast pocket intercepted me. "I'm Donald McKinley," he said, "anything I can do for you?"

"No, thanks," I said, "we're here for the ten o'clock funeral. I know the room."

"Well," he said, looking straight at Vernon and Arthur, "there is a rule here, like most funeral places . . . what's your name?"

"Aaron Broom. I have a rule too. My friends and I honor those of us who die. That's your business, isn't it? To honor the dead?"

"Yes," he said, flustered, "but there is—"

"Good. That's what we're going to do." We went right by him. "Goin' onto the flame," Arthur mumbled, "we's all the same." McKinley made a few gurgling sounds but did not follow us into the room.

We were eight in all now, not counting Augie, and I felt good that we were there for him, sitting in that group of straight-back wooden chairs. Augie got up and faced us.

"Thank you all for coming," he said, "to help a stranger say goodbye to his father. He was a

fine man, did good things in his life for the people around him especially my mother and me.
His love for my mother was a beautiful thing but
when she died it left a hole in him that couldn't
be filled. Then without her there to help him as
he began to lose everything, to keep him from
giving up and being defeated and broken down,
I tried to help him, honest I did, but he lost
his spirit, lost everything. But during the good
years, all the solid things he taught me will stay
with me and help me all my life. May God bring
him peace."

He turned to the coffin, took one last look at
his father, placed his hand on his chest, then
slowly brought down the lid of the coffin. He
leaned his forehead against the polished top and
let his mind send a final farewell.

We all sat in prayerful silence, heads down, as
Vernon began to sing very quietly, Arthur join-
ing him, softly harmonizing:

Shine the light, brother
Light up the way
Shine the light, brother
Light up the way
Shine the light, brother
Light up, light up the way

Augie picked up his head and faced them. Vernon and Arthur stood up, locked arms.

All the way, brother
Through night, through day
All the way, brother
Through night, through day
All the way, brother
Light up the way
He's comin'
He's comin'
He's comin' to stay
Praise the Lord, brother
He's comin' to stay

Two attendants came in and wheeled the coffin away. I got to my feet and said, "Augie, you're now facing the unknown, but you're not facing it alone—your father's soul is with you. That note he left you to marry well and if you have the good fortune of having a son to give him his name so he can continue to love you and be a part of your family, that is his soul, Augie, he is sending you his soul and before his body reaches the fire his soul will be a part of you and your son-to-be. In the short time you and I have known each other, we have been like brothers and I hope in all my heart that your life will reward you for being the fine person you are."

ON THE way out, standing at the door, Mr. McKinley was all toothy smiles. He came to Vernon as we were walking out. "That was marvelous singing," he said, "and I wondered if you and your friend would be available to sing . . ."

We just kept walking.

Happening 32

I went to the Mercantile building early because I was very nervous. I had everything ready for Lawyer Appleton but there was no way of knowing if my stuff would be good enough for him to do something lawyerly for my father. I took his card out of my pocket and rubbed my fingers over the raised letters of Gary, Appleton and Bishop three times for good luck. If Lawyer Appleton decided there was nothing he could do, I really had no one else to turn to. That I had Lawyer Appleton giving this much time and attention to my problem was a miracle, and I know how lucky I am to have come this far, but this is it. Nothing else I can do.

WHEN THE lobby clock showed two minutes to five I took an elevator to the twelfth floor and went to Gary, Appleton and Bishop. The same lady behind the desk said, "Hello, good to see you again, Mr. Broom."

That I was greeted and recognized just like that threw me a little, but also gave me some confidence.

"Mr. Appleton will see you shortly. Please have a seat."

I sat longer than the last time and the longer I sat the more anxious I became. There were two men also waiting in nearby chairs, and they were looking at me funny, like what is this shabby little kid doing here? I guess they were big shots who owned big passenger ships or a bunch of freighters.

The woman at the desk said to the men, "Mr. Gary can see you now." They got up and went to the door with his name on it.

The desk lady's phone buzzed and she said, "Yes, Mr. Appleton. Right away." She got up and took some papers into Mr. Appleton's office. When she came out she walked over to me and said, "He'll be with you in a minute or two."

And he was. After several men left his office Lawyer Appleton came out to get me. He was just as friendly as he was the first time. We sat down on the leather couch in his office, and the same lady as last time, I guess his secretary, brought us

Cokes on ice in crystal glasses. Lawyer Appleton raised his glass toward me, we clicked and took a drink.

"You've been a busy fellow have you?" he said.

"Yes, sir. I've been detectifying with lotsa help. I have everything here, stuff I wrote down in my notebook and stuff in my head that I'm going to tell you."

I went through everything from beginning to end. From that first day when I saw my father go into J & J tugging his Bulova watch case, the bullet crashing through the J & J window, the corpse on the gurney going into the ambulance, my father's arrest in handcuffs, the Justin and Joel brothers and their conversation Augie and me overheard at Pete's, Justin getting tossed from the REO into the gutter and me finding his wallet with the name of Catfish Kuger, Matt J. Pringle of J & J who is really Catfish's manager of his places and whose real name is Anthony Aravista, Grace Dorso the plump J & J saleslady who is really Catfish Kuger's disguised wife Graciella Borsolini, Ted Dempsey the dead man who used a gun he wasn't supposed to have but didn't push the alarm button connected to the police he was supposed to push, Bonnie Porter the once Veiled Prophet Queen of Love and Beauty now a J & J saleswoman married to the actor Roy Delray, Sol Greenblatt the J & J watchmaker I followed to his riverfront places, the mysterious flapper in the Marmon convertible, the good chance that J & J is really owned by Catfish. How Augie and me found out most of this when we snooped in Grace's apartment.

He took all my notes, shuffled through them, sat back, and took a good long look at me.

I nearly died. Really. But I didn't blink.

"Aaron, you are a wonderful whatcha-call-it detectifier. How you were able to get all of this beats me. My better judgment tells me I'm not prepared to deal with a criminal matter since all I've ever practiced is maritime law, shipping contracts and accidents, and such matters related to the rivers and the seas, but I so want to help you free your father. I am foolishly going to override my better judgment."

"You will!" I jumped up, almost knocking over my Coke. "Oh thank you, thank you, Lawyer Appleton, thank you a thousand times over!"

"So this is what I will do. I'm going to begin with a writ of habeas corpus, which is a procedure I learned about in law school but never once used in my practice. It's Latin and lawyers keep using Latin to make them sound special. Would you like to be a lawyer, Aaron?"

"Well, maybe like Clarence Darrow, saving all the innocent people from the electric chair, but mostly I think I'm going to be a writer, I've already started my autobiography."

"Good for you. Well, habeas corpus means 'you may have the body.' It's a writ that makes them bring your father into court where the prosecuting attorney will try to convince the judge that it's necessary to keep him in jail until there is a trial and we'll try to convince the judge that there is not enough grounds to keep him in jail."

"We'll convince him all right!"

"And we'll issue subpoenas—more Latin—to each of the people involved in this matter, those people you have in your notes."

"What's a subpoena?"

"It's a summons that makes them come into court for the hearing or else they face fines or jail time. Now this will take a little while—can you get along till then?"

"Oh sure. I have a very nice place at the Eads Hooverville and my friend Buddy Silverstone has arranged for me to give tennis lessons to little kids for ten cents a time."

"Can you get along on that? I'd be pleased to help you out."

"Oh thank you but I'm just fine. Lawyer Appleton, you're a great man doing all this for a boy you don't know who's come to you off the street."

"Well, Aaron, to tell you the truth I had a son just like you, a little younger, his name was Ben. He was our only child. We were great pals, Ben and I. He was funny and loving and smart as a whip. But when he was eleven Ben came down with polio. It was a sudden and terrible thing. He suffered. But not for long. He died quickly. So did five other children in his class. I see some of Ben in you."

"I'm so sorry for you, Lawyer Appleton. Two kids in my class died of polio and one is very crippled."

He got up and I followed him to the door.

"How do I get in touch with you?"

I tore a page from my notepad and wrote Buddy Silverstone's number at the tennis court.

Lawyer Appleton walked me to the elevator. "Keep the faith," he said as the doors opened for me.

Happening 33

I polished up a penny, put it in my sock for good luck, and got to the courthouse way in advance of everyone else. I wanted to observe them as they came in with their subpoenas, which was a word I had to look up to get the spelling. Lawyer Appleton didn't have to subpoena me but he said I would have to be a witness before the judge and swear to tell the truth which made me very nervous, not that I wouldn't tell the truth but one of my failings is that I have a tendency to exaggerate.

There was only one person in the courtroom when I came in, the one called the bailiff, like the one I remembered from that other time I was in court. He was fussing around the judge's desk, putting out the gavel and water pitcher and a desk sign that said "Judge Harley J. Honeywell." I thought his name had a good-luck sound to it.

They all began arriving with their subpoenas around the same time. The J & Js—Joel and Justin—chubby Grace Dorso, Bonnie Porter with Roy Delray, Matt J. Pringle with the beautiful Marmon flapper whose name I found out was Veronica Wister, and Sol Greenblatt. I was sitting in the back row and no one even looked my way. When Lawyer Appleton arrived he came over and sat down next to me.

"Nervous?"

"Well, um, yes, sir," I admitted.

"Don't be. Just be yourself. If the assistant D.A. asks you something you have trouble with, just look at me and I'll help you out."

The bailiff asked those who were there on subpoenas to come down to the front of the courtroom and sit on chairs arranged in front of the judge's bench. I sat beside Lawyer Appleton who put himself at a desk in front of the chairs. Across from him was a similar desk where the assistant district attorney sat. He was a tall, skinny man with a thick black mustache, a pointy Adam's Apple on a very long neck, and bushy sideburns. My stomach froze when I thought of him throwing questions at me.

The bailiff said, "Everybody rise. The court will come to order. Judge Harley J. Honeywell presiding."

The judge was a short man with a full crop of white hair and a ruddy complexion. He smiled at us and told us to sit down. He wore a black suit with a red bow tie but no robe.

"Good morning all," he said.

We all answered good morning.

"This is an informal hearing," he continued, "in response to Mr. Appleton's writ of habeas corpus re the holding of one Frederick Broom as a material witness in connection with an action now pending re the fatal shooting of one Ted Dempsey. Evidentiary rules will not apply, hearsay will be permitted, the court will question witnesses along with Counselor Appleton and Assistant District Attorney Percy Quince. Bailiff, you may bring in Frederick Broom."

The bailiff opened the door behind the judge's bench. My heart was pounding and I jumped to my feet as my father came in whiskered and wrinkled, accompanied by a uniformed cop but no handcuffs. I ran over to my dad and we hugged each other, holding on like we would never be apart again.

Percy Quince got up and objected.

"Object to what, Mr. Quince, a father and son loving each other?" the judge said.

The cop took my dad to a chair just below the judge's bench. Pop was a proper man, always clean-shaven and spiffily dressed, and I had never seen him in a suffering, browsy state like this.

The judge told the bailiff to swear in all of us. The bailiff picked up a Bible and said everyone rise and raise your right hand and do you swear to tell the truth the whole truth and nothing but the truth so help you God.

We all said I do.

The judge said he had read the district attorney's file on the case and was familiar with all the facts so that the only thing before the court was for Quince to prove that Frederick Broom was a necessary witness who must be detained.

Quince went over to where my father was sitting. "Your Honor," he said, "I think it's important to note that Mr. Broom has had trouble with the law and has an extensive rap sheet. He has been arrested three times for theft of electricity, two warnings and the last time resulting in a thirty-day jail sentence that was stayed."

"How did he steal electricity?" the judge asked.

"He jumped the meter in his apartment by unfastening the wires going into the meter and connecting them to the wires on the other side of the meter, thereby cheating the electric company of its charges."

My father spoke up. "We had no money to pay for electric, Your Honor, and—"

"Mr. Broom, you will get your turn to speak when your lawyer questions you," the judge said.

"Thank you, sir," Quince said. "Next, Mr. Broom has secretly vacated apartments he has leased without paying the rent that is owing. Next, Mr. Broom is in serious default on a Ford automobile that he refuses to surrender, defying the replevin court orders to do so. As for the current case, Mr. Broom was involved with the J & J killer in that he helped him enter the store and held his pouch while the killer filled it with the jewelry. Also, prior to going to the J & J store, Mr. Broom instructed his son, Aaron, who was in the aforementioned Ford, to be ready for 'a fast getaway.' "

My father started to protest but Quince cut him off. "Your witness, Mr. Appleton," he said.

Lawyer Appleton got to his feet. "Mr. Broom, did you know the man who pushed in behind you? Had you even seen him before?"

"No, sir, I should say not," my father said.

"Did you ask your son to be ready for a fast getaway?"

"Yes, if he saw the two repleviners and the Ford was about to be taken away."

"You are a naturalized citizen of this country?"

"Yes, sir."

"Is Broom your original name?"

"No, when I came here I spoke no English and the immigration officer said my Polish name was too difficult and said I should change it and he made it Broom."

The judge turned his attention to the J & J people. "Grace Dorso, you were working in the store when Mr. Broom came in?"

"Yes, sir."

"Did you hear or observe anything that would lead you to believe Mr. Broom knew the killer?"

"Well . . . when the killer told him to hold the bag for him, Mr. Broom said something that sounded like 'Okay George.'"

"Anyone else hear that?" the judge asked.

"I think I did," Matt Pringle said. "It was all so fast."

"I didn't hear anything," Sol Greenblatt said. "Mr. Broom's hands were shaking and he looked too scared to utter a sound."

"How about you, Bonnie Porter?" the judge asked.

"Yes, yes I heard him say something but I was way too nervous to know just what he was saying."

The judge turned his attention to Roy Delray. "Who are you, sir? Were you in the store?"

"No, Your Honor," Roy said. "I'm her husband and I can tell you she was a bundle of nerves that evening and told me the killer and Mr. Broom were in cahoots."

"Aaron Broom," the judge called out, causing me to nearly pee in my britches, "how old are you?"

My voice felt stuck in my throat but I managed to quack, "Almost thirteen."

"You know you've sworn on the Bible to tell the truth?"

"Yes, Your Honor, I always do."

"Good. Before he left the Ford to go into the J & J store did your father say anything about meeting someone to go in with him?"

"No, sir."

"Did he say anything about getting some diamonds?"

"No, sir. Just about selling some of his Bulova watches."

"Did he tell you anything about picking someone up in the Ford when he returned from the store?"

"No, sir. Nothing like that."

Quince came over to me. "Did your father usually tell you about his plans, like who he was seeing for business?"

"No, I only kept watch in the Ford but he just got this Bulova job so there wasn't much to talk about."

"Had he made any sales?"

"No, not yet."

"So your dad needed money?"

"Sure, like everyone else."

"Did your dad talk about teaming up with someone to make some money?"

Lawyer Appleton stood up. "Your Honor, I protest this kind of fishing expedition with a twelve-year-old boy."

"It is too vague, Mr. Quince," the judge said, turning his attention to Justin and Joel. "Were either of you in the store when this event took place?"

They said they weren't. The judge asked them about the value of the stolen jewelry.

"We're working on that with the insurance

company," Justin said. "At least five or six hundred thousand."

"Mostly diamonds?"

"Yes, Your Honor."

"Mr. Broom," the judge said to my father, "the detective on this case reports you are not cooperating with information about the killer who you aided in taking the jewels from the case. Therefore, in view of the testimony from Grace Dorso, Matt Pringle, and Bonnie Porter that you seemed to be acquainted with the killer, I'm impelled to continue to hold you as a material witness."

I jumped up knocking over my chair. "Oh, no, Your Honor, please, can I, I mean, may I tell you some things that are very important? Please!"

Lawyer Appleton put his arm around my shoulders. "Judge," he said, "I took this case because this remarkable boy has applied himself and uncovered some things that I believe will affect the disposition of this case."

Percy Quince jumped up. "This is ridiculous, Your Honor, a twelve-year-old boy—"

"Your Honor," Lawyer Appleton said, "may I have a few moments to talk with my client?"

"Go right ahead," the judge said.

With his arm around my shoulders, Lawyer

Appleton guided me to the back of the court-room and through the swinging doors out into the corridor. He squared me up and said, "Take five deep breaths." I did. "Easy does it," he said. Then he smiled at me and walked me back.

Happening 34

Proceed, counselor," the judge said to Lawyer Appleton when we returned. Then he turned to me. "Come up here, young man, and sit in this witness chair."

"Your Honor," Lawyer Appleton said, "I'd like to request the presence of a court stenographer so that this testimony is on record."

The judge summoned a stenographer from an adjoining courtroom and I hiked up the steps and sat in the big chair that was behind a little gate. The judge told Lawyer Appleton to proceed.

"Aaron," he said, "please state your name, age, and address."

"My name's Aaron Broom, I usually live with my mother and father at the Tremont but now I have a hammock at the Eads Hooverville."

"You're there by yourself?" the judge asked.

"Yes, Your Honor, the cops have locked up our apartment and my mom's in the sanitarium."

The judge turned to the bailiff. "Lou, contact Juvenile Welfare on behalf of this young man."

A voice from the rear of the courtroom said, "We're already on it, Your Honor. We tried but weren't able to locate him."

"Who are you?" the judge asked.

"Freda Muller, Juvenile Welfare."

There she was, marching down the aisle in her boogeyman outfit with her briefcase at attention. It was strictly up to me now to convince the judge to free my dad or Doomsday Freda's going to get her hooks in me.

"Good," the judge said. He nodded to Lawyer Appleton. "Counselor, let's proceed."

"Aaron, you came to see me about what you could do to free your father, didn't you?"

"Yes, sir, and you told me the only sure way was to discover who the killer was and that's what I've been doing—detectifying."

"You've been what?" the judge asked.

"Investigating all these people," Lawyer Appleton said, "connected with J & J jewelers where the killing took place to try to find anyone who may have been involved with the killer. So, Aaron, tell Judge Honeywell about your detectifying."

"I started with Sol Greenblatt, followed him to his places on the riverfront. He told me a lot of things about everyone at J & J and something else—that J & J had a panic button in back of the counter that went right to the police and if there was a robbery that was to be used, not a gun."

"What can you tell the court about Joel and Justin Jankman, the owners of J & J?"

"I heard them say they took all the big important diamonds and put fakes in their place in order to make a good deal with the insurance company but that they were worried because the killer now only had the fakes and he could maybe make a deal with the insurance company but the brothers needed the money to pay off someone they were afraid of."

"No name?" Lawyer Appleton asked.

"No name."

Justin and Joel jumped up and began to shout about needing a lawyer and I was just a snotty runt of a crazy kid, etcetera. The judge gaveled them and told them to sit down and shut up.

"You may resume, counselor," he said.

"Aaron, did you find out who the Jankmans were afraid of?"

"Yes, sir," I said. "How it started I was on the

sidewalk in front of J & J detectifying when a black REO sedan came by suddenly and pitched Justin out the door and into the gutter. He was all beat up and torn and Augie, who sold newspapers on the corner, helped me get him to Pete's speakeasy back room. I found his wallet in the gutter and there was a card in it that said Catfish Kuger with a telephone number."

"What did you do next?" Lawyer Appleton asked.

"We went to the *Post-Dispatch* morgue and looked at photos and right there in a photo of Catfish was Matt J. Pringle, well, not exactly, he had some changes to his face but it was him all right, with his real name on the photo— Anthony Aravista."

Pringle stood up. "Okay, yes, I was Catfish's lawyer but I was disbarred and served time."

"And now he works at J & J?" the judge asked.

"Yes, along with another person," Lawyer Appleton said. "Grace Dorso. Continue, Aaron."

"Augie and I decided to go to her place and interview her but when we got there she wasn't in but her place was open and we went in to look around."

Grace shouted, "It wasn't open. They broke in."

"We didn't break anything. We just looked around."

Lawyer Appleton asked me, "What did you find, if anything?"

"There was a framed wedding picture of young Catfish in a tux with a young, pretty bride who could've been Grace before she beefed up and changed her face all around. I took off the back of the photo and tucked in there was a marriage license." I took my notepad from my pocket and read: "Gaetano Cugavelo to Graciella Borsolini."

"Did you find anything else?" Lawyer Appleton asked me.

"Yes, sir, in Grace's desk we found the *River Princess* account book that showed a big dollar number for Roy Delray. When my friend Ella and I went to see his wife, Bonnie Porter, she said he often performed on the boat and we thought it might have been his pay."

"What made you change your mind?"

"It was a little thing but I was on a trolley and I saw a big fat guy hurrying to get on, coming toward me, and I noticed the way he was walking. He was very fat, his fat legs rubbing together, not at all like the fat shooter at J & J who stepped very lightly behind my father and left the store quickly and springily. So it dawned on me maybe the killer wasn't that fat."

"Meaning what?"

"Maybe he was a skinny guy in a fat suit like Santa Claus wears and a false beard and everything else. But this was no ordinary getup. It could have fooled anybody, the beard, hair, everything."

"Did you keep on looking?"

"I had to. All that stuff about Catfish and Grace and Pringle didn't turn up the killer and my dad would stay in jail until they found him. So I tried to locate the place where the killer may have gotten the fat suit and beard and all the rest. I went to Scruggs and found the department where they had recently sold a supersize shirt and overalls but the saleslady couldn't remember who bought it."

"What happened next?"

"Well, something lucky happened. I went with my friend Ella to interview Bonnie Porter. She's married to the actor Roy Delray who was playing Falstaff at the Muny in *The Merry Wives of Windsor.* Her father was a big shot who had been the secret Veiled Prophet at one time in the past and Bonnie herself had been the Queen of Love and Beauty at the Veiled Prophet Ball. She gave us free seats. I had never seen this play but when Roy came on all decked out in Falstaff's huge fat suit, a bell rang.

"The Muny kept its costumes under lock and key so he couldn't have gotten it there. I also went to the Veiled Prophet place to find out about the huge Veiled Prophet costume but they were so secret they wouldn't even talk to me."

Roy Delray stood up and walked to the bench yelling this was absolutely ridiculous, listening to a punk kid, why would he do anything like this, he had good income what with the radio program and acting and we are prosperous people!

The judge banged his gavel and the bailiff went to Roy and led him back to his seat.

"Not another peep out of you, Mr. Delray, this is not a free-for-all, understand?" the judge said.

He turned his attention to me. "Young man, I know you want to help your father but—"

Lawyer Appleton cut in. "If it please Your Honor, the witness has one last thing to relay. It's something he told me this morning."

"All right. Final say."

"I was lying in my hammock last night," I said, "looking at the sky when it came to me:

The Veiled Prophet shut me out and said only Veiled Prophet members can come in but Bonnie Porter is a Veiled Prophet star, she was once the Queen of Love and Beauty, she's certainly a member, so that's how Mr. Delray got his fat suit and wig and beard—"

Bonnie turned on Roy. "I told you they'd find out! You wouldn't listen! They know! They know!"

Roy jumped up, pointing his finger at Pringle and yelling, "It's all his fault! He said that his goon would break my arms if I didn't pay up pronto!"

"You gamble on the boat and you pay or you pay the price!" Pringle shouted. "Catfish warned you!"

"It was crooked! Cheats! A crooked, rotten boat! That's why I had to steal the diamonds, to pawn them, to get your blood money—"

"These were all orders from her!" Pringle shouted as he turned to face Grace.

"It's not me," Grace said to the judge. "Catfish is the one who gives the orders when I go visit him. His goons keep an eye on me, making sure everything goes to Veronica."

"But you don't give me all I got coming,"

Veronica Wister, the Marmon beauty, chimed in. "The two of you steal from what he wants me to have."

"You're lucky to get what you get," Grace said. "I'm his wife. I'm the one deserves——"

"But I was more to him than you ever were."

"You were what? His sometimes tootsie, his toy."

"You're all a bunch of crooks, pushing in on us," Justin said, "muscling in on our store——"

"He said I would get the store," Veronica told the judge.

"He did not!" Grace protested. "As his wife I was the one——"

"Baloney! Catsy said, 'Honeybunch, it's your nest egg until I buy my way outa here.' "

The two women were on their feet now, facing each other. Grace gave Veronica a big push, knocking her down. "That's a lie! A lie! You were nothing to him! Zero! Just a tart——"

Veronica, back on her feet, grabbed Grace and both of them hit the floor clawing at each other. Sol, Joel, the policeman, and the bailiff tried to separate them as the judge pounded his gavel so hard he broke the handle in two while bellowing, "Order in the court! Order in the court!"

It all finally subsided, the ladies were put back on their chairs, their dresses kinda torn and their hair messed up.

Percy Quince went up to the judge. "Your Honor, the district attorney and his staff are on their way. Everyone must remain in place until they arrive." The cop pulled out his gun.

Lawyer Appleton spoke up: "Under the circumstances, Your Honor, I request the discharging of Mr. Frederick Broom."

The judge, who was applying his handkerchief to the perspiration on his face, said, "Granted."

So Lawyer Appleton and my father and me walked out of the courthouse and onto the sidewalk. I turned to look up at Lawyer Appleton's tall face that was smiling down on me. I took his hand and shook it.

"You are a wonderful man, Lawyer Appleton."

"You are, sir," my father said.

"This meant as much to me as it does to you," Lawyer Appleton said. Then he opened the door of his car that was parked at the curb.

"May I give you a lift?" he asked.

"You already have," I said.

He got in his car and smiled at me through his window as he drove away.

"Let's go to Gino's and have a good Italian lunch," my father said. "Then we'll get Bertha and go see Mother."

"Sure Dad, but could we please go to Garavelli's instead of Gino's?"

Happening 35

As soon as we finished lunch, a treat for both of us, my father was eager to go get Bertha and drive to Fee-Fee, but as we were passing a shop I made him stop and look at the two of us reflected in the window. "Mom sees you with your scraggly beard and the suit you've been wearing and sleeping in all this time and me rumpled as I am, well, just look at the two of us in the window— she'll faint."

"Oh my God," he said, taking a good look. "They didn't have a mirror in the jail. Let's head to the apartment and make ourselves beautiful."

Riding the streetcar with my pop after the wonderful lunch at Garavelli's, where he talked the most I ever heard him talk, made me doubly aware I wasn't dangling on my own anymore. I fought my way up the mountain, now I'm coasting down the other side.

THE POLICE SIGN was gone from the door along with the locks, and my booty was safe and sound in the Fatima tin. While Pop attacked his beard, I indulged myself in a hot shower with a head-to-toe dowsing of Lifebuoy soapsuds; all the crazy things that had happened since the J & J shot was fired seemed to wash off and float down the drain.

Before leaving to get Bertha, as my father poked through the mound of bills and throwaways, he found two important-looking letters, one from Bulova that said it had received the sample case that had been returned from the J & J jewelry store where my father had deserted it. For such negligence, the letter said, he was herewith fired. So there went our only hope of being able to pay some of those bills, but the other letter put back that hope since it was from one of the new groups called the Work Progress Administration being started by President Roosevelt. "Dear sir, we are pleased to inform you that your application has been approved. Your contact in the St. Louis office is as follows . . ."

"Fired and hired just like that."

———

WHEN WE picked up Bertha from behind the mountain of tires at the used-parts place, the owner said the engine was still pretty good but that all four tires were frazzled and had to be replaced, the windshield wipers were shot and so were the brakes, and the radiator leaked water.

"Well," my father said, "to tell you the truth my son and I are going to have trouble scraping up gas money but as soon as I start my new job at WPA, I'll be coming here to take care of good ol' Bertha."

The way he said "my son and I" I knew my Fatima hideaway cash was in trouble but so be it, I got my pop back and I'm perfumed with Lifebuoy.

WE HAD to stop twice on the way to Fee-Fee to water up the leaking radiator but that didn't dampen our enthusiasm for seeing Mom, both of us scrubbed and pressed. When we reached the enclosure beneath where her bed was, however, the bed was empty. *Empty!* I grabbed on to Dad. "Oh no! Oh no!" he exclaimed. I was too shocked to make a sound. Frozen I'd say. Pop said he would go ask at the desk and I should stay put. But as he started away there was a loud knocking on one of the half-open windows that got our attention and it was Mom who had now improved to the walk-arounds which meant she'd be coming home soon.

We had a great back-and-forth and I dropped a few tears of joy seeing her in a pretty summer dress having happy talk with my father even though it was somewhat difficult making themselves heard with so many people on the lawn talking up to patients. So the feared moment of death became a moment of joy.

Happening 36

The WPA people said it would take about three weeks to process my father, salary not yet determined, but in the meantime he was to report to the WPA instructional group. We had very little money, virtually none in the family bank, which was a cookie jar over the stove. As I had guessed, my Fatima hideaway cash was scooped up for the gasoline that got us to Fee-Fee and back. The loot I had in the band of my felty plus the little Pop had in his wallet could get us a few groceries, but what about the apartment rent (in serious arrears), the pile of sanitarium charges, and the electric and gas bills (no more funny business jumping the meter)? It was at that moment, sitting alone at the kitchen table, letting the Depression blues wash over me, that the bell rang. I looked through the peephole and saw a policeman. What now? I suffered a stab of panic—what to do? Maybe not answer, maybe run out the back door, but go where? The bell rang again. They know I'm here, probably have the back covered. Prepared for the worst, I opened the door. The policeman wasn't alone. There was a man with a camera, plus two men in suits.

"Are you Aaron Broom?" the cop asked.

"Yes, sir," I said. My knees were castanets.

"We'd like to come in."

I said, "Sure, come on in."

My mind was absolutely boggled. The living room, with my Murphy In-A-Dor in the wall, was pretty small and the group filled it up.

"Aaron," the cop, who had stars on his collar so he must have been a lieutenant or captain, said, "I have this citation for you from the mayor of St. Louis." He unrolled a scroll he had in his hand and read it to me while the cameraman took pictures. "The City of St. Louis salutes Master Aaron Broom for his fortitude in bringing vital information to the authorities resulting in the arrest of a murderer and criminal charges against individuals committing unlawful acts. Signed Bernard F. Dickmann, Mayor." He opened up a little box that had a pin in it that he fastened on my shirt. It was ebony with gold letters that said "Honoring Valor" and under the lettering was the shield of the City of St. Louis.

One of the two suits took the officer's place beside me while the camera guy clicked away. "Aaron," he said, "I'm George Rogers of the Reliable Insurance Company. It's my pleasure to present you with this reward check for five hundred dollars as offered to the public by our company. It is public-spirited young men like you that keep our country safe." He shook my hand and handed me the check. Sure enough: five hundred dollars, a five and two zeros.

The other man was taking notes in a *Post-Dispatch* notebook, and now the photographer asked all of them to get around me for a group photo. I was absolutely whirling like I'd been stuck on the Flying Turns at the Forest Park Highlands.

They all shook my hand and patted me on the back and left, except for the *Post-Dispatch* reporter who stayed awhile and asked some questions, writing down what I said in his notebook.

After he left, I took the mayor's tribute and my five-hundred-dollar check and my valor pin and went to the bathroom mirror to look at myself displaying them. It brought a great big smile to my face. No doubt about it, Hilda Levy's soul was around, reminding me to always expect the unexpected.

When you go from two quarters in the liner of your felty to five hundred dollars snug in your pocket, plus your picture on the front page of the *Post-Dispatch*, it's like a deep-sea diver coming up too fast and getting the bends. We learned all about that when we studied anatomy. I thought that with my mug in the *Post-Dispatch* everyone would rush up to me asking for my autograph but actually nobody at the tennis courts or on the streetcars paid any attention to me.

But who did bust with pride was my father who carried my picture around and laid it on each and every person he met, whether he knew them or not. Embarrassing.

The paper was full of all the Catfish connections, like the gambling *River Princess* and Pete's and the jewelry store, all of them being run from Dannemora with the help of Matt J. Pringle who was Anthony Aravista and Grace Dorso who was his wife, Graciella Borsolini, but I had no interest in reading about what was going to happen to them. I was through with all of it and that was that.

MY DAD was head-over-heels dedicated to throwing a birthday party for me. For all the Depression years I hadn't had a birthday party because everything that's a party—cake, candles, costumes, presents, music, games, clothes, friends—was in zero supply when you go to eleven different grammar schools and the landlords are trying to evict you. But now with all the bills tidied up and Bertha reborn, thanks to the Reliable Insurance Company, Pop was putting up some paper decorations and getting into the swing of it.

I had received in the mail a splendiferous birthday card my mom had made in the therapy section at the sanitarium, making it doubly sad she wouldn't be at my party. Also, it was sad that Augie wasn't there but he sent a card and wrote that he was glad to be in Keokuk working alongside his cousin's three sons raising cucumbers and pickling them in barrels of brine and selling them to grocery stores. Not my cup of tea, so to speak, but good to know it was a fit for him. I sent him a nice letter and enclosed a generous hunk of my reward loot. I also sent a shiny new smokeless stove to Vernon and a gift card for the Mound City Liquor Store to Arthur.

THE DAY of my birthday was as hot as any other but Pop borrowed a big fan and put it in the window and I guess it helped some. He gave me a nice card and his prized silver pocketknife that his father had given him. I was very moved by that but when I went to hug him he just shook my hand. I also got a card from Lawyer Appleton that said, "If one day you decide to go to law school I have a place reserved for you."

Ella and Mrs. McShane were the first guests, bringing paper plates and a pot full of that special chili con corny and a T-shirt that said "You're the Best." Buddy Silverstone showed up with an almost-new Bill Tilden tennis racket that he had strung himself. He also brought his phonograph and some records. Buddy started the music with "Pennies from Heaven" and that got everyone singing and dancing around. The party was in full throttle when Vernon and Arthur arrived, Vernon with a carrot cake he had baked and covered with peanuts. Arthur had a covered wicker basket that he left outside the door. Pop served cold drinks he had invented and it was simply the best party anyone ever had anywhere, with Ella leading the singing with her beautiful voice, Buddy dancing with Mrs. McShane, and Vernon and Arthur beating out the rhythm.

I pulled Ella aside for a moment and told her my best present was being able to give her a long-lasting supply of that epilepsy medication that I had obtained at the drugstore. She gasped and hugged me and we both shed a couple of tears with our cheeks pressed together.

Mrs. McShane served buns with her plates of chili con corny and everyone sopped up the gravy, wiping off the paper plates.

Vernon put his cake in the middle of the table and decorated it with thirteen plus one candles that he took from his pocket. He took out his lighter and started to light the candles, he and Arthur counting them out loud one after another with number fourteen to grow on.

With all the candles glowing on the cake, Vernon said, "Ready, get set with your wish, goodbye to twelve, hello thirteen, fire up your wish and we'll all make wishes for you, ready—go!" I got all the candles with one big blow-around and

Ella plucked the candles as Vernon sliced pieces of cake for everyone and Pop poured more of his drinks.

I'll tell you how I felt. For the first time, I felt that I truly belonged somewhere. As the peanuts from the delicious cake crunched under my teeth, I felt real love in that room. Luck, detectifying, and especially the helping hands of strangers had gotten me over the hot coals of those mean times, strangers who are now true friends.

Arthur made a bugle call with his hands cupped over his mouth and carried in the basket he had left outside the door. It was tied with a huge blue ribbon. He put the basket on the living-room table and presented it to me. I had no idea what might be inside. I untied the ribbon and slowly raised the wicker lid as a yelp came from within and a golden retriever puppy poked her head over the basket's edge. Everyone clapped with delight as I picked up the puppy and snugged it to my face.

"Arthur!" I said. "Where in God's name did you get such a—"

Vernon cut me off. "If you don't mind, lad, Pickles don't like to palaver 'bout his acquisitions. He has his own mysterious ways."

"She ain't got a name yet, that's up to you. There's some puppy kibble and toys in the basket," Arthur said.

I put the puppy down and Ella gave her a bowl of water which she lapped up happily. She made a joyous round of everyone in the room.

"I'm going to call her Hilda," I said, picking her up and rubbing noses with her. "Welcome, Hilda, welcome."

Happening 38

It was the first morning of my thirteenth year and I was taking Hilda for her first walk, she strutting proudly on the end of the yellow leash I found on the bottom of Arthur's basket. As we turned the corner onto DeBaliviere, there was Nathan's pawnshop with its three gold balls gleaming in the sun. The window was packed with a variety of objects, primarily musical instruments: violins, a banjo, ukuleles, an accordion, a drum set, a flugelhorn, but there also was a shelf that contained jewelry, and I tried to see if my mother's brown diamond was among the rings on display.

While I was concentrating, with my nose pressed on the window glass, the door opened and Nathan himself stuck his head out.

"Come in, Aaron, come in. It's not too often we get a celebrity outside our window. Your father came in yesterday carrying the *Post-Dispatch* to brag about you."

I had met Nathan that time my father had taken me along when he was pawning something. I liked seeing the things in the shop, some of them pretty weird, that people had pawned; pawning is a sad business and I felt sorry for them, especially my father who, I could tell, was suffering when he handed over what he had brought for Nathan's money.

But, listen, that is not to say that Nathan was anything like Shylock in *The Merchant of Venice* that we'd studied in Hilda Levy's class. Nathan was a cheerful man who liked to tell corny jokes and laughed with the kind of laugh that made *you* laugh. He had been friends with my father a long time and he told my father he wouldn't sell his stuff, especially the brown diamond, unless he absolutely had to. Nathan was a nicely dressed, handsome man, nothing like the picture of Shylock in our Shakespeare book.

If I had not haphazardly turned onto DeBaliviere, it would have never occurred to me to think about the brown diamond and what it meant to my mother and father—all those arguments, for selling it or keeping it. Now with my father getting a job guaranteed by President Franklin D. Roosevelt, my mother about to come home all healed up, and me with a wad of dough in my pocket, even after taking care of the back rent, Bertha's tires, wipers, radiators, and crumples, the refrigerator chock-full, plus some stuff on the shelves in the kitchen.

"Is that the pin?" Nathan asked, inspecting my shirt. "Honoring valor," he read aloud.

Hilda decided she had been ignored long enough and she pawed Nathan's shoes. He picked her up and she slurped his nose. "Who have we here?"

"Say how-de-do, Hilda. She was a birthday present yesterday."

Hilda slurped him again and yipped twice.

Nathan opened a drawer with his free hand and took out a small red pocketknife that he handed to me. "You have a knife?"

"No, sir, never did."

"Now you do. Happy what?"

"Thirteen. I've always wanted a knife. Thank you. Thank you very very much."

Nathan put Hilda back on the floor.

"Mr. Nathan," I said, "looking at all these things you have here, you've certainly helped a lot of people, my father being one of them, and it's wonderful how so far you haven't sold our brown diamond."

"I know how much it means to your dad, but

to be honest, if I get a bona fide buyer, I'll have to sell it. Your dad is way past due to redeem it."

"How much is due?"

Nathan opened a big ledger book. "One hundred and forty."

"Tell you the truth," I said, "I'd forgotten about the brown diamond until now. I still have a little of my reward. I was going to give it to Mom when she comes home, so she wouldn't have to worry about food and the lights and the streetcar and gas for Bertha for a while, but what I'm thinking is maybe, just maybe, that brown diamond on her finger means something more important. Maybe it's a part of the way they love one another. I don't much think about love, but what do you think? That's what people do. They come in here, don't they, and give up things they love? And sometimes, if they're lucky, they can buy it back and it makes their lives feel better."

"Well, Aaron," Nathan said, "it's true, I am in the business of buying things desperate people love, and although I try to be as fair as I can, I do know the moment hurts them when they give me the object and I hand them money to replace it. I have no family, never married, but I know."

At that very moment, I felt a funny kind of yearning travel through me. Like I said, I never thought much about love. I had never said the words to anyone. And yet it was there, I guess. I could see myself returning that ring to my parents. I could feel their joy, my mother's tears, my pop holding her. I was tearing up a little and I turned my face away from Mr. Nathan so's he wouldn't notice.

I put my hand in my pocket and took out my rubber-banded money and started to count out the price of the ring.

"Make that an even one hundred," Nathan said.

There was not much left but I felt really good, like that day we won the championship baseball game and my teammates hoisted me up on their shoulders and paraded me around.

Nathan polished up the ring with a special cloth and put it in a little velvety box. He put his arm around me and walked us out the door. But before we took off to continue our way to Forest Park, Hilda made a good-luck puddle in front of the pawnshop where there was a leafy sycamore tree.

E pluribus unum.

ACKNOWLEDGMENTS

I first met Nan Talese, my editor for this book, fifty-four years ago, in the office of Bennett Cerf, the cofounder of Random House. I had written *Papa Hemingway,* a memoir of my long friendship with Hemingway that Bennett was publishing, my first book, and Bennett had asked me to come meet the editor he had assigned to it. I had gone to Cerf's office hoping that the editor would be one of his "name" veterans, but who came to join us was a most attractive, quite young woman I thought was an intern who was going to lead me to one of those "names." Not so. She turned out to be the perfect editor for my book and for me, with an instinctual understanding of the man I was writing about. She did not intrude, she guided and suggested, asked questions that took me beyond what I thought were the limits.

Over the intervening years, Nan has been my editor on many books, bringing her skills and insights to the betterment of each and every one of them, this one included. We have also shared a close friendship, as I have with her husband, Gay Talese. That's how it should be. A fine editor really does become family, and, I'm proud to say, Nan has.

———

In so many ways, my wife, Virginia, was a steadying, helpful influence during the challenging, chaotic time it took me to write this book, as she has been on my other books, even contributing one of my favorite titles: *O.J. in the Morning, G&T at Night.*

3-10-20
4-20-22
    1 (CHQ)

3/10/20